A GAME OF
AUTHORS

A Game of
Authors

Frank Herbert

 WordFire Press
Colorado Springs, Colorado

A GAME OF AUTHORS
Copyright © 2013 Herbert Properties, LLC

ISBN: 978-1-61475-076-5

Book Design by RuneWright, LLC
www.RuneWright.com

Published by
WordFire Press, an imprint of
WordFire, Inc.
PO Box 1840
Monument CO 80132

WordFire Press Trade Paperback Edition November, 2013
Printed in the USA
www.wordfire.com

CHAPTER 1

Hal Garson, a tall, blond young man with deep-set blue eyes beneath bushy brows, stepped off the Mexican National Railways' train from Guadalajara, plopped his suitcase in the yellow dust.

Ciudad Brockman—here the search really begins, he thought. And then: *The trouble with Antone Luac was that he was too good a cynic. People are of two minds about a successful cynic: they admire his wit, and they fear his attention. A successful cynic can't just disappear. People secretly want him to come to a bad end—and they want the gory details.*

The somber look of Ciudad Brockman caught Garson emotionally. It lay brooding and silent in the siesta-time heat, crouched against a dun-colored mountain like a last stronghold of feudalism held at bay. The mountain formed a threatening backdrop for the city profile of orange roof tiles and jagged steeples.

The look of the place was fitting, all of a piece with the letter from Eduardo Gomez Refugio. The letter had come to Garson in Seattle, forwarded through a magazine that had published a Garson short story about a Mexican *brasero* in the United States.

"Dear Ser: I rid you history in magzine all aboat good Mejicano werk in Unitd Stados. I want much to go Unitd Stados for brazero werk. Now I werk for bad man gangster from Unitd Stados. He is sicret in Ciudad Brockman. He esend meny brazero to Unitd Stados. Never esend mi, Eduardo Gomez Refugio. I giv all history to you ser when you esend mi United Stados for werk brazero. Plis to be very sicret aboat letter to you. He kill mi. You come to Ciudad Brockman and see I spik truth werds. You ask at Tintoreria Nueva York my cousin Lalo. He to tell mi when you say it and nobody lern. For truth my wards I esend letter of gangster to see his fingerprints for F.B.I. of Unitd Stados. Also his name.

Yours affectionately,
Eduardo Gomez Refugio"

Enclosed had been a sheet of bond paper, and on it in a small script a shard of prose—beautifully simple, tantalizing for its incompleteness; a satiric love scene between someone called Elena and someone called Harold. On the back of the sheet was a signature in the same hand: *Antone Cual*—and what looked like a grocery list in Spanish.

The prose and name carried an odd sense of familiarity to Garson. And the letter with its air of conspiracy, its plea for caution and secrecy, made him chuckle.

But there had been something pathetic about the Mexican's plea—a story behind the letter's labored English that told of a struggle to conquer an alien tongue with nothing more than a dictionary and possibly a phrase book.

Garson's atlas showed Ciudad Brockman more than 3,000 miles south of Seattle, deep in the Mexican state of Jalisco. Much too far away for the answering of a plea from a half-illiterate Mexican. The letter and enclosure were touched by mystery, but not worth an expenditure of time by a professional writer whose working hours were mortgaged to previous commitments.

He was on the point of filing the letter under unfinished business—in case he ever *happened* to visit Ciudad Brockman—when his gaze again rested on that neat, concise signature: *Antone Cual.* Garson's eyes made a sudden reversal of direction, and the impact of what he saw brought a tremble to his hand as he bent over the paper.

Cual is a simple anagram on Luac! he thought.

He got out the correct volume of his encyclopedia, found the reference:

"Luac, Antone: born Slagville, Iowa, March 21, 1884. Began newspaper career Chicago, Ill., 1908. Reported Mexican revolution 1912–13 for New York Herald. Went to Europe for Associated Press at start of World War I. Returned January 1919 to career as novelist. His better known works: *A Handbook for Heaven and Hell, Downright Ditties, Choose Your Weapons, The Kaiser's War.* Luac disappeared in Mexico in August, 1932, in company with Anita Peabody, wife of his friend, Alan Peabody, San Francisco drama critic. Peabody later obtained a divorce, naming Luac correspondent. Several attempts to trace the couple have failed. This is considered one of the celebrated disappearances of the Twentieth Century (See also "Famous Missing Persons" by George Powell Davis.)"

Garson found his copy of *A Handbook for Heaven and Hell*. The prose from the mysterious letter carried the same casual, biting simplicity.

The fire of discovery began to burn in Garson. He called his agent in New York, explained about the letter from Mexico. His agent caught some of the same fire. Two days later, Garson had a promise from a national magazine to underwrite part of the expenses for an investigation, or to pay all of the expenses if the story proved true.

That was how he found himself standing beside a railroad track in Mexico, staring moodily at Ciudad Brockman.

His eyes detected a cross on the mountain like a white hole in the blue sky. It prodded his memory of the city's history learned from his quick research. The cross testified to the Latin passion for monuments to human agony. General Brockman's peon legions had held out on that mountain top against ten times their number of Spaniards. Two years of death, torture, and cannon shells for the men on the mountain while the Spanish soldiers lived with the defenders' women in the city.

The mountain and city seemed to say to Garson: "We have seen passion, misery, death and tears before. What is one more story of these things to us?"

A nervous laugh at such dark thoughts escaped Garson. He looked around for a taxi.

Ahead of him a cobbled avenue lined by scarred, dusty trees and high-walled cornfields stretched across the valley floor toward the city and overhanging mountain. The avenue carried traffic of two slow motion burros and a peon. Muddy plaster peeled from the walls lining the avenue, half obliterating the splashed red paint of election announcements.

Over it all, the sun, like a giant ember, seared everything to dusty silence.

To Garson's left under the open shed of the railroad station, Indians sat on benches—men with huaraches on their feet, dirty white trousers, and the hand-embroidered white shirts they wore to market; the shawled women in black or Carmelite brown dresses, like brooding hens, like pieces of the earth. Children played in the dust beside tethered pigs and chickens. Some of the Indians slept with their heads tilted back, faces hidden beneath straw sombreros. Others stared silently at Garson.

They saw the *gringo* cut of his clothes, the harsh jaw line, the air of purpose about him. From these things the cinema-steeped Mexicans built a picture of something secretive and official. Before nightfall they were telling each other that he must really be an American secret agent come to investigate the local mystery: the Hacienda Cual.

There was no sign of a taxi. Garson wondered if he would have to walk the sun-scorched avenue. At every other station in Mexico he had been overwhelmed with offers of service. Here, no one approached him.

Then, a group of Indians standing with their backs to him near a wall at the far corner of the station moved aside. Garson saw the hood of an automobile. He stepped forward to get a better look, and the car moved away from the wall.

It was a black limousine with a wooden box newly roped onto the rear. But Garson's attention remained fixed on the young woman in the rear seat. She had reddish auburn hair, large eyes of a darkness that seemed to trap the light, a complexion like translucent alabaster that—in this latitude— spoke of seclusion, of an old-world custom that hid the fair virgins behind high walls and alert duennas.

As the limousine moved past him, the woman turned, stared directly at Garson. She seemed to catalog him and discard him all in the time that it took her long lashes to flick once over her eyes.

The limousine turned up the avenue, gathered speed. And only then did Garson's mind—assembling the other elements of the scene—tell him that the man beside the driver had worn crossed bandoliers, studded with cartridges, and held a rifle sternly upright.

And Garson thought: *I'd disappear in Mexico myself for something like that!* And for the first time, it occurred to him to ask himself: *Just what did Anita Peabody really look like? Was she as beautiful as that?* The newspaper pictures he had seen—faded and with the woman appearing somehow lumpy in the flapper costume of the era—had left Garson dissatisfied.

A church bell began tolling in the city: a hollow, off-key sound that echoed from the mountain. And now, a pinch-faced boy ran around the station wall, stopped in front of Garson. The marks of Spain and the New World were pressed into the boy's features as though by a sculptor with a heavy thumb.

"*Libre, Señor?*" asked the boy.

"*Libre*" translated to "taxi" in Garson's mind. He said, "*Si.*"

The boy jerked Garson's suitcase from the ground, led the way at a dog trot through the silently staring Indians. On the opposite side of the station where the limousine had been there was a telephone. Soon, a taxi appeared on the cobbled avenue, bouncing and careening as it sped toward them.

The El Palacio Hotel was a one-story building, tile-floored, dim and cool behind a deep arcade that fronted on a garden plaza. The lobby held three rows of tables that could have been transplanted unchanged from a New York soda parlor, circa 1900. They were marble-topped, set in spindle-legged wrought iron baskets. The chairs had the same unsubstantial twisted-wire appearance.

Two delicatessen cabinets flanked the hotel's registration desk. The glass fronts of the cabinets revealed rows of bottled beer, American process cheeses, and slabs of Spam.

The clerk was a dark-skinned little man with bright hard eyes, a delicate line of mustache, and the hawk beak of a grandee.

He wrote a room number after Garson's signature in the heavy register, said, *"Gabriél Villazana, a sus ordenes, Señor."*

Garson's mind did its usual slow-motion translation, noting that the clerk had identified himself as Gabriél Villazana.

He gave his *when-in-doubt* answer: *"Gracias."* The clerk nodded, waved up an urchin who staggered along beneath Garson's bag.

The room was at the end of a hall off the lobby. It was a high-ceilinged space with a half wall in one corner separating shower and toilet. The light came from a skylight directly above a brass spool bed that sagged in the center. There was a mildewed smell about the room. Garson noted that a pile of dead crickets had been swept into one corner.

Gabriél Villazana handed Garson a heavy iron key for the door, accepted his tip with a swift motion of hand into pocket, produced a yellow envelope from another pocket.

"Para usted, Señor."

Garson took the envelope, saw that it was a telegram addressed to him at "El Mejor Hotel de Ciudad Brockman."

The best hotel in the city. He grinned, tore open the envelope. It was from his agent:

"The Times morgue says Anita Peabody secretary-treasurer of Friends of the Poor: on first list of front organizations. Branches in Mexico. Maybe this helps. Maybe it only confuses. Good hunting."

Garson re-read the telegram. *Something to do with the communists in this?* And he thought of the bitter cynicism behind Antone Luac's writing. *Not a chance! Luac was an incipient royalist. He'd spit in the Reds' eyes!*

He tossed the telegram onto the swaybacked bed, decided to use the siesta time for a shower, shave, and change of clothing before seeking out his contact at the *Tintoreria Nueva York*—The New York Dry Cleaners.

It turned out to be a day of half-accomplishments for Garson. And the telegram kept returning to his mind, nagging at him. He wondered if there were a secret message in the telegram—something urgent his agent felt that he must know.

Or why would he send a telegram?

He decided finally that it was the brooding atmosphere of mystery about Ciudad Brockman causing his uneasiness. But he still did not feel satisfied.

The Tintoreria Nueva York was directly across the garden plaza from the hotel. It fronted on another arcade behind a mosaic walk. The *tintoreria* had once been a residence. The patio glimpsed through a half open door behind the long wooden business counter had a cracked fountain, rows of potted plants.

Eduardo Gomez's cousin was a blond, Germanic type— round cheeks, a sunburned complexion, small eyes, a personality like an adding machine. What did not add up to money for this man did not exist. He gained interest only when Garson—with the aid of a phrase book—said that he had *business* with Eduardo Gomez.

Through frequent reference to the phrase book and a pocket dictionary, Garson presently understood that Eduardo Gomez possibly would be in town that day—possibly the next day—possibly the following week—or perhaps not for a month.

Garson turned the conversation to the Hacienda Cual, saw the cousin mentally retreat. A door seemed to close behind his eyes.

A customer entered the *tintoreria*. The cousin excused himself.

Garson returned to the hotel, feeling his uneasiness intensified.

What did Eduardo Gomez write in his letter? "He kill mi." *Could there be something in that?*

Gabriél Villazana, the hotel clerk, was disposed to practice his high school English. He was also less inhibited on the subject of the Hacienda Cual.

"*Sí, Señor.* Un mystery. Very big mystery." He leaned across his registration desk. "The trucks, *Señor.*"

"Trucks? What trucks?"

"Every three, four months, *Señor.* They come. They go."

"What's in them?"

Gabriél Villazana shrugged. *"Quién sabe?"* He cocked his head to one side. "Perhaps you are interested in the *Señorita* Cual, *Señor.*" His eyes rolled heavenward. "Ah, *Señor.* She is a mango!"

It turned out that a "mango" could be literally translated as "a dish." Garson immediately recalled the queenly young woman in the limousine.

The conversation turned to the peace and beauty of Ciudad Brockman. Gabriél Villazana emphasized that there had not been a gun fight in the plaza for almost two years.

Garson registered appropriate admiration, returned to the subject of the Hacienda Cual. "Is it far from here?"

"No, *Señor.* One hour by car." Abruptly, he stared at Garson with a look of shock. "But you are not thinking of going there, *Señor?*"

"Why not?"

"They kill you, *Señor!*"

"Huh?"

Gabriél Villazana became excited, lapsed partly into Spanish with bits of shattered English.

There were guards at the hacienda. Very fierce guards. People disappeared. When one approached the Hacienda Cual there were warning shots—then... Again, the expressive shrug of the shoulders. And the *Señor* Cual, the old man, he had important friends in the government.

Garson tried to get a description of the *Señor* Cual.

It was sufficient for the clerk that the old man of the hacienda had a distinguished face, white hair, and a small beard on the chin that Garson decided must be a goatee.

The incomplete description was another of the afternoon's frustrations.

Garson excused himself.

Gabriél Villazana had one more thought. "Do you have a gun, *Señor?*"

"Of course not. Why do you ask?"

"There are people who do not like those who ask questions about the Hacienda Cual. Perhaps you would like to buy a gun, *Señor.* I know a man who sells them."

"I think not. Thanks anyway."

Again, the shrug of the shoulders.

Garson returned to his room to rest until dinner time. He felt immensely tired, blamed it on the altitude.

Maybe Eduardo Gomez will actually come to town today, he thought.

But he did not really believe it.

"*Señor!* Hssst! *Señor* Garson! Hssst!"

Garson awoke. His eyes looked upward to the skylight of his hotel room. A pale mauve sunset color tinted the opaque glass.

For a moment, he had no idea where he was. Then he remembered: Ciudad Brockman—El Palacio Hotel. He recalled taking a shower in the afternoon heat, deciding to nap before going out to dinner. At the thought of food, his stomach pained him like a child yowling for its supper. He lifted his wristwatch from the bedstand, found that he had been sleeping more than two hours.

What awakened me? Hunger?

Again his stomach constricted.

He could hear a low-voiced conversation in Spanish outside his door. Then "Hsssst! *Señor* Garson!" The voice was high pitched with an air of nervousness.

"Who is it?"

"It is Eduardo Gomez Refugio, *Señor.*"

Garson said, "*Un momento.*" And he thought: *For crying in the dark! He did show today!*

He got up, slipped on a pair of trousers, ran a hand through his hair as he opened the door.

A thin, dark-haired man in a poorly cut navy blue copy of an American business suit stood at the door. The man had eyes like varnished grapes, fearful and subservient. His manner suggested an inner war between servility and self-assertion. He spoke with a grave, comic dignity, a faint bowing of the head.

"*Señor* Garson, I have the honor to be Eduardo Gomez Refugio at your service."

Garson saw Gabriél Villazana, the clerk, behind his caller. The clerk nodded, returned to the front of the hotel. Garson stepped aside.

"Come in. I was just taking a nap."

Eduardo Gomez glanced behind him, entered the room. "*Sí. Sí. Con mucho gusto.*"

Garson closed the door, turned to Gomez. "You speak English, I see."

Gomez stared at him. Then: "Eenglays? Sí, *Señor.* I espeak."

"Well… uh… glad to meet you." Garson held out his hand.

Gomez shook hands with a single, chopping motion. His palm felt hard and calloused. "I esmae, *Señor.*"

Silence settled between them.

Garson felt uncomfortable under the steady examination of the other's eyes.

"I got your letter, Mr. Gomez. And I…"

"*Sí, Señor.* The letter."

Garson had the distinct feeling that Gomez now regretted the letter. There was an air of tragedy about Gomez, a sense of inevitable pathos.

"I'd like to meet this *Señor* Cual," said Garson.

Gomez glanced at his wristwatch. It seemed a motion designed to point out that he owned a watch rather than an actual interest in the time. He returned his attention to Garson.

"You esend me to Uneeted Estados, *Señor?*"

"That's part of the bargain."

The varnished grape eyes looked to the door, back to Garson. "Please not use name of gahngster. Very danger. Many spies. Ciudad Brockman bien full of spies."

"Okay. But can I see this man?"

"I drive automovile of her *señorita* today, *Señor.* Tonight, I come. We espeak."

Garson started to reply, but his memory nudged him to an abrupt silence. He realized that he had seen Eduardo Gomez before, that this thin little man had been sitting behind the wheel of a limousine at the railroad station.

"The *señorita*," said Garson.

"La hija, Señor."

The daughter! Luac and Anita Peabody have a daughter!

The realization that the daughter was the queenly beauty of the limousine did nothing to reduce Garson's excitement.

"What time will you come?"

Gomez stared at him without comprehension.

He speaks English like I speak Spanish!

Garson gestured to his own wristwatch. "La hora?"

Gomez nodded. *"Sí, Señor. Está la hora.* Tonight I come. You get all history."

"Yes, but…"

"No talk to any mens, *Señor.*" Gomez went to the door, peered out, turned back to Garson. "Very danger."

It dawned on Garson that Gomez was about to leave. The Mexican confirmed this by saying "*Adiós, Señor.* I go with God."

Garson held out a hand. "Wait!"

"*Sí, Señor.* You wait."

With that he was gone, the door closed quickly and softly behind him.

Garson crossed to the door in two steps, opened it, looked out. Most of the lobby tables were occupied. He caught one glimpse of Gomez as the man stepped into the arcade.

I go with God. Such a curious air of tragedy about the statement. Garson experienced a creeping sense of menace, of premonition. He felt that the little man's words might haunt him.

He closed the door, finished dressing.

A warm darkness filled the street outside the arcade when Garson emerged. He stepped from the lobby into a flow of people. There was a new spirit about everyone. Children ran up and down the arcade, whirled around the posts that fronted on the street. Voices were lighter, swifter, as though relieved of some pressure known only to the day.

Ciudad Brockman's mood of sad brooding had disappeared with the coming of night.

"You're the newcomer." It was a deep voice speaking at Garson's shoulder.

He turned, confronted a tall, heavy man with the most ferocious face he had ever seen. The skin was pockmarked, knife-scarred, burnt almost black by the sun. His eyes were like two hunting animals lurking in slitted caves. A wide straw sombrero shaded his face from the arcade's yellow lights, creating an effect of concealment. The man's mouth was a thin slit beneath a handlebar mustache, his chin blunt and square. The nose had been broken and mashed.

"I admit I'm not pretty," said the man, "but it's not polite to stare."

Garson felt his face grow hot. "I'm sorry," he stammered.

"Don't be." The man held out a blunt hand. "I'm Carlos Medina. Call me Choco."

Garson shook hands, felt a casual, almost brutal strength in the other's grip. "I'm Hal Garson."

"Pleased to meet you, Mr. Garson." The English was spoken with easy confidence, totally without a Spanish accent. "What brings you to Ciudad Brockman?"

Garson parried the question. "You sound like someone from the chamber of commerce."

Choco Medina smiled, revealing even, gleaming white teeth. "That's true in a way. I'm an interpreter, and I have a car for hire. I make my living from visitors."

"Not many gringos come here, do they?" asked Garson.

"No, not many."

"You speak excellent English," said Garson.

Medina shrugged. "I was born in El Paso, grew up there and in Juarez."

"Oh." Garson studied the battered face, wondered at the instinctive liking he felt for this man with the evil features. "It just might be that I could use a car and interpreter. What's the rate?"

"Five pesos an hour, twenty-five pesos a day." Again he smiled. "That's for interpreting. The car is one peso a kilometer."

Garson converted twenty-five pesos to dollars at the current exchange: two dollars.

"That's pretty cheap, Mr. Medina."

"In dollars, maybe. But it's the local rate."

"Okay. You're hired."

"When do I start?"

"How about right now?"

"Fine. What are we doing?"

Garson sensed that there was more than casual interest in the question, said, "I'm a writer. I'm here to research the material for a magazine article."

Medina nodded. "Good." He gestured toward the hotel. "Let's get a beer in the lobby here, and you can tell me about it."

Gabriél Villazana served them at one of the marble-topped tables, appeared to focus with an abrupt recognition on Garson's companion.

"*Buenas tardes, Gabriél,*" said Medina.

Villazana's head bobbed like a puppet's. "*Buenas tardes, Choco.*" He backed away, turned, almost ran to his counter.

Medina raised his bottle to Garson. "*Salud.*"

"*Salud.*"

The beer tasted cool and tangy. Garson drained half the bottle, put it down, said, "I see you know the clerk."

"We're acquainted."

"He seemed a little afraid of you."

"Maybe I was too rough on him when I asked about my brother." Medina stared at Garson as though expecting a response.

"Am I supposed to say something?" asked Garson. "What about your brother?" He put the beer bottle to his mouth.

"Someone murdered him."

Garson choked on a swallow of beer, coughed. "Sorry." He stared at Medina. "Did Villazana have something to do with it?"

"I don't think so. But he was in Torleon when it happened."

"Torleon?"

"The little town about ten kilometers south of here. It has a good bullring. My brother was murdered on a Sunday—in the crowd coming out of the plaza after the bullfights."

"Who did it?"

Medina leaned back in his chair, shook his head. "I don't know. I wasn't there. I have only one clue—from the daughter of an old man who was hit by a car and killed on the day after my brother was murdered."

Garson wondered why he was being told these things, said, "What's the clue?"

"The nickname of the triggerman. The old man evidently saw only the back of his head, but he heard him called '*La Yegua*.' That's a common nickname for bad-tempered people. It means 'The Mare.'"

"Was the old man killed to shut him up?"

"That's my guess."

"This is very interesting," said Garson. "I'm sorry, of course, to hear about the tragedy in your family."

"Perhaps you can use it in your story, Mr. Garson."

"I doubt it."

"What *are* you going to write about?"

Again Garson sensed that something important hung on his answer. He decided to try for maximum effect. "I'm going to write about Antone Cual. That's not really his name, though.

It's Antone *Luac*, the famous writer who disappeared in Mexico in 1932 with another man's wife."

Medina remained impassively calm. "That's a dangerous assignment," he said.

"Why?"

"The hacienda is well guarded."

"Why?"

"Perhaps to keep out such as yourself."

Garson smiled. "He's never been up against me before."

"Do you carry a gun?" asked Medina.

"I won't need a gun." And he thought: *I've never met that question before in my life but here—twice in one day!*

Medina pulled back a flap of his jacket, revealed a heavy revolver in a belt holster. "I carry this for *La Yegua*." He closed his jacket, leaned forward. "Allow me to explain some of our quaint customs. Here in the back country, two out of three people carry a revolver. They are either like me: gunning for someone; or they are afraid someone is gunning for them."

"So?"

"So bodies are occasionally found, Mr. Garson. It is not a rarity. In fact, it is sufficiently common that the police are not too zealous in finding out who pulled the trigger."

"Do the police know you're carrying a gun?"

"Undoubtedly, but they try not to know it officially. No cop wants to buy in on somebody else's feud. This is asking for trouble."

Garson realized abruptly that this was part of the atmosphere that had produced the air of musical comedy melodrama in Eduardo Gomez's letter. He said, "Are you trying to warn me off?"

Medina shrugged. "I merely point out one of the obvious difficulties in your path."

"Thanks. I think I'll go ahead anyway. The American Consulate knows I'm here. Maybe the police would be more zealous in my case."

"We can hope there will be no case, Mr. Garson."

A chill passed over Garson. He reacted with a nervous laugh, said, "I'm just a writer. People don't go around killing writers—*poof!*—just like that!"

"The story going the rounds is that you're a secret agent."

Garson stared at him, shocked. "That's crazy!"

Medina smiled. "Mexicans try to make a mystery out of everything. If there's no mystery, they manufacture one. Sometimes, the mysteries they manufacture are better than real ones."

"But why are they interested in me?"

"Because you've been asking around about the Hacienda Cual—and that's already a favorite mystery here."

"So you already knew why I was here?"

"I've learned not to trust Mexican rumors."

"What are the rumors about the Hacienda Cual?"

"There are so many I wouldn't know where to start."

"Well, it's no mystery, Mr. Medina. It's…"

"Please call me Choco."

"Okay, Choco. The Hacienda Cual is really a very simple matter. It started with a love story—a man and a woman."

Medina raised his eyebrows. "Hell! Everything starts that way!"

Garson laughed, glanced at his wristwatch, was surprised to find it almost seven o'clock.

"Are you expecting someone?" asked Medina.

"No. I'm going to eat dinner and knock off for the night. I can't seem to get enough sleep."

"It's the altitude. You'll get used to it."

"Unless I'm forced to get used to a much higher altitude first."

This seemed to strike Medina as funnier than Garson had expected. The Mexican guffawed, attracting the attention of people at surrounding tables.

"Maybe you don't think writers should go to heaven," said Garson.

Medina wiped a tear from his right eye. "You should write humor, Mr. Garson."

"Perhaps I should."

The Mexican sobered, leaned far back in his chair. "What time will you want me in the morning?"

"Will eight o'clock be all right?"

"Good enough." Medina pushed away from the table, got to his feet. "Then, if you won't be needing me anymore tonight…"

"See you in the morning," said Garson.

Gabriél Villazana came to Garson's table as soon as Choco Medina was gone. "That is a very bad man," said Villazana.

"I suppose so," said Garson. "But I kind of like him."

Villazana's shrug seemed to say that he had done what he could, that all gringos were crazy anyway, that after all only a confirmed idiot stands in the path of fate.

CHAPTER 2

The sound of someone scrambling on the roof above his hotel room awakened Garson from a light sleep. He opened his eyes, stared into darkness. He could see a faint moonglow through the skylight. Something like the shadow of a man passed across the skylight. Again, he heard the scrambling sound. A heavy sense of menace filled Garson. He closed his eyes, tried to fight it off, blaming the highly spiced foods of his dinner.

A bright light flicked across his face, visible through his eyelids. The sense of menace was an imminent thing. Garson rolled off the bed.

Something crashed through the skylight, thumped onto the bed. The springs creaked and groaned. Pieces of glass fell all around Garson.

He lay quietly on the floor in the dark, his heart thumping.

Good God! What was that?

He put out a hand, felt on the bed. His fingers encountered a rough, cold surface like rock or concrete.

Footsteps pounded on the tiles outside his door. Someone knocked. Gabriél Villazana's voice came through the panels: "*Señor Garson? Está bien, Señor?*"

Garson remained mute, his throat dry.

An excited conversation in Spanish went on outside his door.

Why don't I say something? Garson asked himself. And part of his mind said: *Because that was no accident! Right now it's safer to play dead.*

Garson got to his feet, took his watch from the bed stand—eleven-thirty.

Then: *Somebody tried to kill me!*

Reaction set in, and Garson's knees began to tremble.

Again, running footsteps sounded on the tiles outside, heavier footsteps. A fist pounded the door.

"Hey in there! Are you all right?"

Garson recognized Choco Medina's rumbling voice.

"Yes. I'm all right," Garson said. He swallowed to ease the dryness of his throat, made his way around the bed, opened the door.

A ring of faces filled the hallway. Garson recognized Medina and Villazana.

A sense of defenseless loneliness filled Garson.

Medina's evil features relaxed into a grin. "You gave us a scare," he said. "What was all that commotion?"

Garson found the light switch on the wall beside the door, stood aside. He didn't trust his voice.

Medina entered. Villazana followed, closed the door behind him.

"Whew-eeee!" said Medina.

"*Madre de Dios!*" said Villazana.

A large, jagged chunk of concrete lay across his pillow, shards of glass all around it. The concrete was easily as long as the pillow, half as wide.

He looked up at the skylight perhaps twenty feet above the bed. An irregular hole reached across the glass. Pieces of the frame hung down, swaying lightly.

"That thing would've crushed your skull like an eggshell if you'd been in bed," said Medina. "Where were you when it fell?"

"Somebody awakened me by making noise on the roof," said Garson. "Then they flashed a light onto my face. I rolled off the bed just before that thing fell."

Again he looked at the chunk of concrete, shuddered.

Medina turned to Villazana, spoke in a burst of Spanish too rapid for Garson to follow. Garson caught the word for workers in Villazana's reply.

"He says there were workmen up on the roof today repairing the wall between this building and the next one," said Medina. "He thinks they must have left that piece of concrete balanced on the scaffolding."

"Then who flashed that light on my face?" asked Garson.

Medina looked at Garson. "Do you think this was not an accident?"

"No."

"Neither do I," said Medina. "But it would've looked like an accident. There'd have been no inconvenient investigation."

"Who'd want to do such a thing?" asked Garson.

"Someone who doesn't like people asking questions about the Hacienda Cual."

Garson studied Medina's pockmarked face, wondered: *Could he have had anything to do with this?* He looked at Villazana.

"The patron saint of this hotel, she was with you tonight, *Señor*," said Villazana. "Ahhh, those bad fellows! I will punish them tomorrow!"

And could he have had anything to do with it? wondered Garson. Villazana did not appear particularly disturbed by the incident.

Garson turned back to Medina, the feeling of wrongness strong in him. "Do you have any idea who could have done this?"

Medina shrugged. "It has a certain familiar pattern, but *quién sabe?*"

"Who?"

Medina shook his head. "I dunno." He glanced up at the skylight, and Garson noted that his hand was close to the revolver in his belt holster.

"Someone like your *Yegua?*" asked Garson. "Someone who shoots from hiding?"

Medina's attention snapped back to Garson. He stared into Garson's eyes with a curious intentness.

"That's a connection I'd never made before," said Medina. "But now that you mention it…" He reached out, snapped off the light.

Villazana gabbled something in Spanish.

"*Callaté!*" rumbled Medina.

Shut up!

"What's wrong?" asked Garson.

"Our friend may still be on the roof," said Medina.

Garson shivered. "Shouldn't we call the police?"

"Don't be a dope," said Medina. His voice sounded like a rolling of gravel in the dark. "Cops can be bought cheap down here. They carry guns that can go off by accident while you are standing unfortunately in the way!"

A feeling of desperate anger swelled in Garson. "Do you have a spare gun, Choco?"

Medina remained silent a moment, then Garson heard him move, saw the faint ghostly shadow of him approaching. Something cold and smooth was pushed into Garson's hand: a revolver.

"It's a thirty-eight special," said Medina. "Do you know how to use it?"

Garson oriented the gun in his hand. "Yes."

"I think you'd better come home with me tonight," said Medina.

The anger became a feeling of stubborn determination in Garson, reinforced by the feeling of the revolver in his hand. "No!"

"This could have been an accident," said Medina. "But I…"

"*Sí!* An accident!" babbled Villazana. "The workmen! They…"

"*Callaté!*" said Medina.

Villazana fell into abrupt silence.

"We'll move the bed out from under the skylight and get Villazana here to put a piece of canvas over the hole," said Garson.

"A piece of canvas won't stop a killer," said Medina.

"I don't think they'll try again tonight."

"What if they don't think the same way?"

"What can they do if I'm not under the…"

"'What can they do?' he says." Medina put a hand on Garson's arm. "They can poke a gun through that hole up there and put a nice new bullet in you."

"I don't think so," said Garson. "That wouldn't look like an accident."

"But you would be just as dead!"

"I'm an American citizen!" barked Garson. "They can't go around popping off an American citizen without a big stink!"

"You know, Mr. Garson, I've run into this strange attitude before. It gets hundreds of American citizens killed every year."

"Besides, I've got a gun now," muttered Garson.

"American citizen with a gun," said Medina. "The world's most dangerous game!"

Garson fought down laughter that he knew would have sounded almost hysterical. "They wouldn't have rigged an accident if they just wanted me dead."

"You can't be sure," said Medina.

"This Antone Luac wants his privacy pretty badly," said Garson. "I wonder why."

"Wouldn't it be a good idea for you just to forget all about this and go home?" asked Medina. "After all, if…"

"What do you mean?"

"Well… one story can't be worth all of…"

"The hell it isn't!"

Garson thought about dropping the story, about leaving this threatening atmosphere of mystery. Nothing had ever sounded so appealing to him. But the anger pulsed in the back of his mind. He felt the weight of the pistol in hand. And something more: the thing he called "story fever." It filled him with an absolute hunger to unravel this mystery.

"Hell no, I'm not going home!" he said.

"It's your funeral," said Medina.

There was a tone like regret in Medina's voice. It sent a shudder of fear through Garson, but he suppressed the feeling.

I'm staying, he thought.

After Medina and Villazana had gone, Garson waited in darkness while someone climbed to the roof, nailed canvas across the shattered skylight. Then he moved his own bed to a corner across the room.

Now that he was alone, questions came crowding into Garson's mind.

What was Medina doing around here so late at night? He was too available. And why did my comment about the killer of his brother surprise him?

And Garson remembered Eduardo Gomez.

Good God! Gomez was coming back tonight! What if he saw all the commotion and got frightened off?

And another, more chilling thought: *What if the people who dropped the concrete saw Gomez visit me today? If they'd try to kill me, would they hesitate over killing a Mexican?*

Again Garson experienced a sense of tragic premonition about Gomez. And he recalled the line from Gomez's letter:

"He kill mi."

Why would Luac kill to maintain his privacy? Garson asked himself. *Why?*

Garson had the sensation that his tight little Stanley-and-Livingstone-plus-female story was getting away from him.

Before the sleep of exhaustion overcame Garson that night, he recalled Villazana's statement about the trucks that visited the Hacienda Cual. *What's in those trucks?*

He slipped into a dream of an endless line of trucks driven by repetitive Choco Medinas. And as each truck passed, the dream Medina looked at Garson with a feeling of deep regret—and shot at him with the big revolver.

CHAPTER 3

Choco Medina awakened Garson at seven the next morning, rapping lightly on the door. "You in there?"

Garson came instantly awake, his first feeling one of surprise that he had actually slept. He could feel the hard lump of the revolver under his pillow. It brought back the full memory of the previous night.

Could it really have been an accident? he wondered.

Again the rapping sounded on his door.

"Hssst! Are you all right?"

Garson recognized Medina's gravelly voice, said, "Yes. I'm just getting up."

"They start serving breakfast out here in fifteen minutes."

"Be right with you."

Garson went first to the hotel desk where an older, white-haired man with a face like wrinkled leather and eyes of veiled caution stood in Villazana's place.

The old man informed Garson that no one had called for him during the night.

Medina, a thoughtful expression on his ugly face, sat at a table near the arcade, his back to the wall. Garson joined him.

"Choco, how do I get out to the Hacienda Cual?"

Medina put a finger to his long mustache, said, "Are you aching to get draped over a fence in a dead condition?"

"Nuts! I've a story to do. The best way is to go right in the front door."

"And out the…"

A hotel maid bent over the table, interrupting Medina. "*Dispense, Choco,*" she said. "*El llave?*"

Garson recognized the word for "key," saw a key pass from Medina to the maid. She crossed the lobby, opened a padlocked door with the key, exposed steps leading upward.

Medina said, "I don't like any part of…"

"Just a minute, Choco!" Garson studied him a moment, looked in the door the maid had opened. She reappeared with a light pallet and a roll of blankets.

"I thought so," said Garson. "You stayed on the roof last night, Choco."

Medina shrugged. "So I made love to the maid."

"Hah!"

"Maybe I was protecting some poor Mexican from an American citizen with a gun. How do you know?"

"I appreciate it all the same," said Garson.

Medina coughed, cleared his throat.

Garson felt deeply moved, a sense of warmth and kinship with this evil-visaged Mexican. He said, "Maybe I'll get a chance to…"

A horn blared in the street.

Both men turned.

The long black limousine of the railroad station stood in the street, the same queenly beauty in the rear seat. A string of pack burros loaded with sacked charcoal blocked the street.

Again the horn blared. Garson's attention went to the driver, noted that it was not Eduardo Gomez but the man who'd sat beside Gomez holding a rifle.

Medina said, "Do you know who that is?"

"Luac's daughter. What's her name, Choco?"

"Anita Carmen Maria."

"How do you know her full name?"

"It's on her baptismal record."

And Garson thought: *Anita Luac—Anita Peabody. Another link in the chain.* He filed Medina's familiarity with the woman's name for future investigation, pushed himself away from the table.

"Where're you going?"

"Out to meet the…"

The limousine found an opening beside the burros, sped off down the avenue.

"It would be safer to go out and tangle with the fence riders at the hacienda," said Medina. "That was José Gomez driving. He's known as El Grillo: the cricket. That's because he can shoot crickets on the wing with his rifle."

"Gomez," said Garson. "Is he related to a man named Eduardo Gomez?"

"Eduardo is his nephew. Why?"

"I'd like to find Eduardo Gomez and talk to him. Do you have any idea where the car may be going?"

"*Quién sabe?* Sometimes they go to the doctor, sometimes to a store, sometimes to the market."

"Choco, see if you can find out where they're going now."

"Look, why don't you stop asking for a casket! This is…"

"Stop this *menacing Mexico* routine for five minutes," said Garson. "This is a straightaway love story—romantic runaways, all the trimmings. That exquisite creature in the car is the love child to top it off!"

Medina shook his head. "You may not respect your skin, but I have the greatest re…"

"Then I'll go find them myself!"

"No!" Medina jerked to his feet. "If it must be, it must be! But you're asking for big trouble!"

"This is just a simple little story of…"

"Nothing is really simple," said Medina. "Wait here for me. I'll do what I can." He went out into the arcade, strode around the corner to the right.

Garson ordered breakfast, ate in a mood of deep thoughtfulness.

Something about Medina doesn't fit, he thought. *Is someone paying him to sidetrack me and frighten me off? And if so—why?*

A familiar horn sounded from the other side of the garden plaza. The limousine came around the corner, stopped diagonally across from Garson beneath a sign that identified the telegraph office. The woman got out, entered the office.

Garson saw no sign of Medina.

He stood up, went to the corner, crossed in front of the limousine. The driver, a dried-up gnome of a man with a pinched face of undersized features, studied Garson with pale eyes that seemed to measure everything they saw.

Anita Luac was inside the office, bent over a counter, writing on a telegraph blank.

Garson slipped in the open door, glanced over the woman's shoulder at what she was writing, caught his breath. Her left hand covered the name of the person to whom she was addressing the telegram, but the words beneath were in a neat block printing, easy to read:

"H. Garson here. One attempt made and failed. Please advise where…"

She sensed his presence, turned, folding back the telegraph blank to conceal it.

Garson stared down into a face so beautiful that sight of it momentarily drove all other thoughts from his mind. Her wide brown eyes were like those of a trapped fawn, full of the awareness that he had seen the telegram. A soft flush stole across the pale cream skin. Her full red lips were slightly parted. A sharply indrawn breath pressed her breasts against her dark blouse.

"You saw!" she said.

Garson felt that her statement was the most terrible accusation. He said, "I, uh…" Then he recalled the words he'd read on her telegram, and a bitter anger filled him.

One attempt made and failed!

"I'm Hal Garson, Miss Luac. Would you like to make another attempt now?"

"This is hardly the…" She broke off, stared at him. "What do you mean?"

"Your assassins missed with that chunk of concrete the other night." He looked up to the cracked plaster of the telegraph office ceiling. "Maybe there's something around here you could have dropped on me."

She glanced at the telegram in her hand, back to Garson. "Oh, but…" She shook her head. "You don't understand. This isn't…" Again she blushed.

"Maybe you'd better explain then," said Garson.

Her lips thinned. "I don't have to explain anything, Mr. Garson!" She crumpled the telegram, turned to leave.

"Miss Luac!" said Garson.

She stopped, spoke without turning. "The name is Cual."

"I have a piece of manuscript that I believe was written recently by a man named Antone Luac," said Garson. "Have you ever heard of him?"

She kept her face averted, stared out at the street. Garson saw the gnome-like driver looking in at her, a question in his eyes. She shook her head at him, and he turned away.

"Have you ever heard of him?" repeated Garson.

"That was a mistake, Mr. Garson," she said.

"I think your father is Antone Luac," said Garson. "I'd like to go out and talk to him."

"My father is old and tired, and desires nothing but peace," she said. "He is not receiving visitors."

"Is your father Antone Luac?"

"I must be going, Mr. Garson."

"But you haven't sent your telegram."

"That, too, was a mistake."

"Tell your father that I'll be out to see him this afternoon."

Her body shook with suppressed emotion. She turned, and her voice came out soft and pleading. "Please, Mr. Garson. This has all been a terrible mistake. Please go away and forget you ever heard of us or of that piece of manuscript."

Garson stared down at her, realizing that she was the most desirable woman he had ever seen.

She held out her right hand. "Please give me that piece of manuscript."

With an odd twisting emotion, Garson knew that he would have been compelled to give her the piece of manuscript if he'd had it with him. He shook his head. "I'm sorry, Miss Luac."

Her face contorted as though she were about to cry, and her voice came out little more than a sob. "Oh, please go away!"

Garson fought to regain his self-control. "Miss Luac, famous people don't have the right to privacy."

She stamped her foot. "That's stupid!"

"I'm truly sorry, but that's the way it is."

She took a deep quavering breath, spoke slowly. "You will not be permitted to see my father. For your own sake as well as ours, please do not try."

Abruptly, she turned away, slipped out to the limousine.

As quickly as she moved, the gnome-like driver was quicker. He was out of the car and the rear door open before she reached the car.

By the time Garson had recovered his senses, the limousine was pulling away. He stood in the doorway, stared after the retreating car.

A deep voice intruded from his left. "Well, now you've met the *Señorita.*"

Garson whirled.

Choco Medina leaned against the wall beside the door. A cigarette dangled from his lips, its coal dangerously near his drooping mustache. A black sedan was pointed into the curb in front of him. Medina pushed himself away from the wall, nodded toward the car. "Shall we go for a ride?"

"Where?"

Medina shrugged.

"How about taking me out to the Hacienda Cual?"

Medina's lids dropped. He spat out the cigarette, stepped on it. "Do you have an invitation?"

"All the invitation I need."

"I will give you odds against it."

"Do you take me, or do I hire a cab?"

"You've already hired me, Mr. Garson. Remember?"

Garson nodded, wondering at Medina's withdrawn attitude. He said, "Did you get a chance to talk to this *El Grillo*?"

"Yes."

"Where's his nephew, Eduardo Gomez?"

"What nephew? He has no nephew by that name."

"But you said…"

"I am quoting him, Mr. Garson."

"What?"

"He suddenly doesn't know anything about a nephew named Eduardo Gomez."

"What's that supposed to mean?"

"Let's go ask him."

They got into the car.

Garson said, "Stop at the hotel a minute."

"Why?"

"Just stop at the hotel."

"You're the boss."

Gabriél Villazana was on duty behind the desk. Garson pressed a twenty peso note into his hand, "Gabriél, I am going out to the Hacienda Cual with Choco Medina. If I'm not back by eight o'clock tomorrow morning, please notify the American Consulate in Mexico City."

Villazana took the money, his hand shaking.

"Will you do it?" asked Garson.

"*Sí, Señor.* But please do not do this. That Choco is a bad man! He will…"

"Just do as I ask."

Garson turned away from him, went to his room. His bed had been made, the room swept. He reached under his pillow and found the gun neatly centered there. A smile touched his lips as he wondered how common a thing it was for the maid to replace a man's revolver when she made the bed. He slipped the gun into his belt, returned to the car and Choco Medina.

"Let's go."

The cobbled street ended at the edge of town, became a dusty, rutted track bounded by rickety fences of twisted limbs. The road wound through fields of sugar cane and corn. Dust thrown up by the limousine ahead of them hung over the ruts.

As the sun climbed, Garson began to feel the heat of the day.

The road angled upward, turning and twisting, bounded now by cacti overgrown with bougainvillea, tall grey-barked trees with shiny green leaves.

Still there was no sign of the limousine except the settling carpet of dust on the road. They came to a fork. The dust trail went left.

"They are going to the upper gate," said Medina. "I don't like that."

"Why?"

He steered the car into the left fork, said, "It is more secluded there."

The turns became tighter, steeper. They rounded a hairpin corner. Medina turned off the road between two stone pillars, braked to a jolting stop as the pinch-faced driver of the limousine stepped into their path, pointed a rifle at them.

The limousine stood parked about one hundred yards ahead beneath one of the grey barked trees.

"Some invitation!" muttered Medina.

"That's El Grillo, isn't it?" asked Garson.

"Yes."

"Maybe I can talk to him." Garson moved to open his door.

Medina gripped his arm. "Stay where you are!"

El Grillo took his left hand from the rifle stock, pointed back toward the city.

"Don't get out of the car for any reason," said Medina. "Just wait right here." He opened his door, got out, walked up to El Grillo.

The rifle remained pointed at the car.

Medina murmured something to El Grillo. The little rifleman glanced back at the limousine, returned his attention to Garson, shook his head.

Again Medina spoke.

El Grillo grinned, looked up for the first time at Medina, shrugged. The rifleman wet his lips with his tongue, said, "Raul?" as though it were a question.

Medina said something too low for Garson to hear.

El Grillo nodded.

Medina returned to the car, slid behind the wheel.

"What the hell was all that?" demanded Garson.

Medina ignored the question, backed the car through the gate, headed toward the city. They rounded the hairpin curve. Medina braked to a stop.

Garson became conscious of the crickets rasping in the dry grass beside the road. They reminded him that the rifleman at the gate was known as "The Cricket." He said, "Okay, Choco. What gives?"

"Are you up to a little hike?"

"To the hacienda?"

"Yes."

"What about El Grillo?"

"He'll take you across the lake after dark for fifty pesos. That's what I was talking about."

"Lake? What lake?"

"You have to cross a lake to get to the hacienda."

Garson took a deep breath. The feeling that there was something deeply wrong with this situation filled him. "How far would I have to walk?"

"About two or three miles."

"Why walk?"

"The riders would hear a car. If you're on foot, you can hide in the brush beside the road when a horseman comes past."

"Am I likely to meet a guard?"

"No. El Grillo said he was the only one on this side right now. He'll meet you where they park the car."

"What'll you be doing?"

"I can't leave the car here."

Garson nodded. "All right. So that's how I get in. How'll I get out?"

"You're awfully cautious all of a sudden."

"I didn't like the looks of that El Grillo."

"He has a price, Mr. Garson. Remember that."

Garson opened his door, got out. "Do I just follow that road we were on?"

"Yes. You can't miss it. Be careful that El Grillo or his Indian woman are the only ones to see you when you get to the barrio at the lake." Medina looked suddenly thoughtful. His evil features drew down into a deep scowl. "There's one other thing."

Again Garson was filled with a sense of danger. "Yes?"

"Whatever you do, don't give away my part in this."

"I don't understand."

"No matter what happens, don't let on that I'm working for you."

"Okay, Choco." Garson lifted his hand in salute.

Medina put the car in gear, pulled away in a choking cloud of dust.

Garson turned, headed back up the road. He felt the weight of the pistol in his belt, brought it out and checked it, stopped in frozen shock. There were no cartridges in it.

Who took them? The maid? Were there shells in it when Medina gave it to me?

He replaced the revolver in his belt, was suddenly thankful that he had made the arrangement with Gabriél Villazana to call the American Consulate.

An acute sense of loneliness swept over Garson. He slapped at a mosquito on his neck, wondered: *Now, what the devil have I gotten myself into?*

The air held a rich smell of earth: moldy, verdant. Gnats and flies buzzed around him. He slipped off his coat, loosened his tie, wished for his hat.

The stone pillars loomed up beside the road. Garson approached them cautiously. No sign of El Grillo. He turned onto the private road, noted that it was little more than a cart track. The limousine was gone.

A flight of yellow and green finches swept past ahead of him, dipped low over the road. Garson quickened his pace, seeking shade. The cart road narrowed, became a wide trail crowded by jungle growth—now shady, now baked in sun glare. A vulture flapped into the air as he approached, settled behind him, waddled off the road. Garson sniffed at the smell of carrion, slapped at the gnats buzzing around his moist neck. He stopped, listened for the limousine, for the sound of danger. Nothing but insect noises.

Loneliness crowded in upon him. He stared into the underbrush.

The vultures would pick a body clean in a day. No one would ever find it. Is Choco pushing me into a trap?

Garson paused, looked back the way he had come, then again up the road.

But then—Antone Luac—and my name on the story!

He shifted his coat to his left arm to conceal the pistol at his belt, continued up the road, moving more slowly, oppressed by the heat, wishing for a breath of wind. Now and again he paused, listening. Only insect sounds.

The road topped a rise, angled downward. It dipped into a heavily wooded area lush with a hothouse smell. He forded a small stream still muddy with the tracks of the limousine, glimpsed an expanse of water through the trees ahead.

The lake?

He rounded a corner, came full into a yucca-walled barrio with the lake beyond. The limousine was parked under an open shed. There was no sign of Anita Luac or El Grillo.

Two hollow-flanked dogs came yapping out at him. A skinny Indian woman in a brown skirt and heavy red blouse ran out of a mud hut in the barrio, kicked the dogs aside, cursed at them.

Garson walked up to her, said, "El Grillo?"

She spoke in a burst of Spanish too fast for Garson to follow.

Running footsteps sounded from Garson's right. El Grillo trotted around a corner of the barrio, slowed to a walk when he saw Garson, nodded. *"Buenas tardes, Señor."*

Garson glanced up, noted that the sun was past the meridian. He said, *"Buenas tardes."* He was struck by the gaunt look of El Grillo. The man wore a white shirt, rope-belted white trousers with ragged cuffs, open huaraches on heavily calloused feet. His face was shaded under a wide-brimmed straw sombrero.

The Indian woman spoke to El Grillo in a high whine.

He cursed at her in Spanish, kicked one of the snuffling dogs, smiled at Garson, and spoke in English with only the slightest trace of an accent. "You made good time."

"I didn't have any reason to loiter." Garson looked at the lake, saw buildings on a point of land across the water. "Is that the hacienda?"

El Grillo spoke without turning. *"Sí, Señor."*

Garson looked down at El Grillo. "You're the uncle of Eduardo Gomez, aren't you?"

El Grillo blinked. Garson had the feeling that the man tensed.

"There is no one by the name of Eduardo Gomez around here, *Señor*." He shook his head. "There is no such person."

Garson recalled his premonition at the hotel.

"I go with God."

He said, "What happened to Eduardo? Did somebody drop something on him?"

"You ask too many questions, *Señor* Garson." El Grillo turned to the Indian woman, spoke in a harsh voice. She went into the hut.

"Is anybody likely to see me here?" asked Garson.

"You must wait until dark," said El Grillo. "The hacienda, as you can see, is on a little peninsula. There is a dangerous swamp behind it. We will go in a canoe."

The sound of a galloping horse came from beyond the barrio. El Grillo took Garson's arm, hurried him into the hut past the Indian woman working at a charcoal fire. They entered a dark sleeping room. The place smelled heavily of perspiration, urine, charcoal smoke, rotting things. A narrow, glassless window opened on thick green leaves. Beneath it was an ancient iron bedstead covered by grimy serapes. Two reed chairs stood against the wall beside the bed.

"You must wait quietly until dark, *Señor*," said El Grillo. He went out the single door, draped a serape in place over it. Garson heard him speak to the Indian woman. Presently, there came the sound of El Grillo talking to a man outside. A horse clop-clopped away.

The stink of the room clung to Garson's nostrils. Flies buzzed around his head. He sat down on one of the reed chairs, brought the empty revolver from his belt, wrapped it in his coat and tossed both onto the bed.

I'm trusting myself to people with hidden motives, he thought. *El Grillo isn't doing this just for fifty pesos. Choco Medina isn't helping because I hired him to do it.* He glanced at his coat on the bed, thought of the revolver. *Who took the bullets out of that thing?*

Garson stared around the room, wondered if there could be bullets hidden here. He inspected the tops of the rafters, peered under the bed, found nothing.

Late in the afternoon, the Indian woman came silently past the serape of the door, handed Garson a plate containing four tortillas wrapped around beans.

He ate in sudden hunger, surprised at the savor of the food.

Afterward, he returned to the chair, turned it so that he could watch the march of the shadow across the muddy ledge of the window. He tried to doze, but couldn't. Several times he stood up, walked to the blanket at the door, hesitated, returned to the window, tried to peer out into the jungle. He decided against stretching out on the bed, reflecting that he would probably share it with too many things that crawled and bit.

And throughout the afternoon, uncertainty nagged at him— a feeling of menace that rode on the insect sounds, the stirring of the Indian woman in the other room, the occasional noises of horsemen in the barrio.

There are too many unanswered questions here, he thought.

Only the promise of breaking the Antone Luac story gave him the courage to stick it out.

El Grillo came at dusk.

"The fifty pesos, *Señor.*"

Garson gave him the money.

El Grillo pocketed it. "Now, we go."

Garson took his folded coat from the bed, felt the weight of the revolver in it, followed El Grillo outside.

Why am I hanging onto an empty gun? he wondered. But the knowledge of it reduced his sense of uncertainty.

It was warm in the dusk outside, with a clinging dampness to the air. Flying insects seemed to be everywhere.

The Indian woman appeared beside El Grillo, screamed at him. He aimed a kick at her. She dodged, continued to scream. Garson heard the name, *Raul.*

"She is afraid Raul will see us and shoot," said El Grillo. He chuckled. "Raul will not see."

"Who's Raul?"

El Grillo remained silent. A breeze stirred around them, carrying the heavy odor of jasmine.

Then: "Raul is a man of much anger, *Señor.* When he is angry, he is dangerous."

El Grillo turned, a ghostly white figure in the gloom, led the way around the barrio and onto a narrow footpath. The trail let out onto the lake—a muddy shore, root clusters dimly visible in the fading light. Swarms of mosquitoes arose from the water. Garson could distinguish the dark shadow of a dock to the right along the shore, the flickering of an open fire among the trees.

"You must be very quiet," whispered El Grillo. "The guards at the dock must not hear." He dropped down to a dark platform, pulled a dugout from the shadows.

Garson scrambled down beside him, found himself on a log raft that gurgled faintly and tipped with his weight.

"You must sit very gently," said El Grillo. He rocked the canoe with a fingertip to demonstrate its delicate balance. "The lake is full of *caribe*. If we go into the water we will die."

"*Caribe?*"

"Little fish, *Señor*. When the *caribe* dine, a man loses his identity."

Caribe? wondered Garson. He looked at the luminous afterglow on the lake, put the thought of dangerous fish from his mind. "Won't we be sitting ducks out there?"

"We will follow the shore. No one will see." He steadied the dugout, motioned for Garson to enter.

Garson took a deep breath, stepped into the canoe, scrambled to the front and sat down in dampness, his jacket and the empty revolver in his lap.

Caribe, he thought. *Could he mean piranha? But they don't have piranha in Mexico. Only in South America.*

The canoe tipped and righted as El Grillo took his position in the stern. The dugout moved out into the lake, turned left along the shore. Garson felt rather than heard the rhythm of the paddle.

Presently, he saw the amber glow of lights ahead. They drew closer. The dugout nosed into a mudbank with bushes bending down overhead.

El Grillo came forward, leaned over Garson's shoulder.

"There is a trail directly ahead of you, *Señor*. Follow that trail. It leads to a wall with a gate. The gate will not be locked. I will leave you now."

"How can I signal if I want you to come and get me?" asked Garson.

El Grillo remained silent a moment, then: "Tie white cloth to those bushes above you there. I will come after dark."

"Will I find your nephew in there?" asked Garson.

"I have no nephew, *Señor.*" The hand pressed his shoulder. "Now, go with God."

Garson felt a sudden aversion to that phrase. He tucked his bundled coat under his left arm, stood up, reached for the limbs overhead to steady himself. There appeared to be a log beside the canoe. Garson stepped to it, slipped. The limbs in his hand bent down. He found himself flat on his back in a foot of surprisingly cold water. With much splashing and floundering, he scrambled onto a mudbank, still clutching his coat, turned.

There was no sign of the dugout. Then he saw a faint movement of white along the shore to his right. It disappeared.

His clothes clung to him with a refreshing coolness. He turned, slipped and scrambled to higher ground, located the trail, paused there while he looked at the lights ahead. They appeared to be windows and some lanterns hung in trees. The weight of the gun and his wet coat pulled at his arm.

Abruptly, Garson slipped the revolver from the coat, found a rotten log beside the trail, pushed the gun under the log, kicked leaves over the area to hide it.

Then he strode toward the lights, his senses alert to every sound.

A low wall loomed ahead, broken by an arched double gate. A gas lantern in a fog of insects hung from a limb just inside the gate. He could see another gas lantern in a screened enclosure beyond the gate.

Almost as though they were lighting my path, thought Garson.

Now, he could make out a high-backed rattan chair in the screened enclosure, a table beside the chair covered with papers.

He stopped at the gate, looked inside the walled area. It was a garden, thick with palms, papaya, mimosa. He could smell jasmine. A brick walkway led from the gate to the screened enclosure, thence to the adobe wall of a house at the other side of the garden.

Garson lifted the latch of the gate, stepped into the garden. Now, he could see a double door in the wall of the house. He stepped out along the walk, froze as a voice came from the high-backed chair in the screened area. It was a man's voice, deep and with a touch of querulousness.

"Is that you, Raul?"

Garson cleared his throat, felt suddenly weak-kneed with the realization that he was at the moment of discovery.

"What's the matter with you, Raul?"

The back of a grey head arose above the chair followed by wide shoulders in a white suit. A gnarled hand fumbled for a cane beside the chair, found it. The man turned.

Garson had seen a hundred photographs of this face: the wide forehead, bulging brows, the thin nose and large dark eyes. Only the goatee was new. It gave him the look of a grey-haired Mephistopheles. There would be no mistake.

This was Antone Luac.

"Oh, so it's you," said Luac.

Garson's voice failed him. He had been prepared for almost any other reaction: for outrage, for bitterness—even for violence—but not for casual acceptance.

"Well, say something," said Luac. "Say, 'Dr. Livingstone, I presume!' or some other damn foolishness."

Garson stammered, "I... I, uh... I'm Hal Garson."

"Who else?" asked Luac. "Well, don't just stand there! Come in out of the bugs."

Only then did Garson realize that many of the insects had deserted the lights to concentrate on his flesh. He saw the door to the screened enclosure on his left, slipped through it. By the time he faced Luac across the table, Garson had regained some of his composure.

Luac sank back into his chair, racked his cane on the arm, indicated a similar chair across from him.

Garson sat down. His wet clothes squished.

"The goatee doesn't change your appearance much," said Garson. "I'd have known you anywhere."

"How did you get so wet?"

A smile touched Garson's lips. "Maybe I swam."

"As the Pharaoh said to his daughter when she explained about the baby Moses: 'Possible but not probable.' Now, while you're busy composing suitable epigrams to record this historic moment, I believe I'll..."

"Antone!" It was a man's voice calling from the house.

Luac frowned, said, "There you are, Raul. Come here. We have a visitor."

A thin, dark man moved catlike around the bushes that hid the house, stopped outside the screened area. His face was oval and with an even regularity of features that was almost feminine. The eyes were wide, limpid with a look of softness. His black hair was combed straight back and with two symmetrical curls, one at each temple.

"Raul, this is the American journalist, Mr. Hal Garson. Mr. Garson, may I present Raul Separdo?"

"How do you do?" asked Garson.

"How did he get here?" asked Separdo.

"He says he swam."

Separdo smiled, displaying even teeth.

Garson had a feeling that the symmetry of this man was a mask to conceal something dangerously out of balance.

"We had best dispose of him immediately," said Separdo.

"Do not be a complete ass!" said Luac.

"Antone! You are playing with something that…"

"I *play* with nothing, Raul! Until we are certain of exactly what he is, we keep him in good condition!"

Garson experienced the chilling realization that he was listening to a discussion of his own life and death.

"Where did he come from?" demanded Separdo.

"That is one of the things I have not yet determined," said Luac. "Until I…"

"Did El Grillo bring him—or one of the others?"

Luac looked at Garson. "Who brought you, Mr. Garson?"

"The stork!" barked Garson. He felt the anger dangerously close to the surface of his mind.

Luac chuckled.

"A wit!" said Separdo. "What a pity that the world must lose this!" He moved around the screened enclosure, entered, took a position beside Luac's chair.

"He does present some problems," said Luac.

"Could he be a member of the American secret service?" asked Separdo.

Garson stared at him.

"One of the thoughts I have considered," said Luac.

"Why would I be a member of the secret service?" asked Garson. And he felt that he had been suddenly immersed in a cloak-and-dagger situation that somehow lacked reality.

Separdo's hand went to his belt, came up with a Luger. "Has he been searched, Antone?"

"Of course not! He just arrived."

"Where's Choco?"

Garson stiffened. *Choco?*

"Inside somewhere," said Luac. "I heard Nita ask him to play a game of cards earlier."

"I don't like keeping this man around," said Separdo.

"But you do not give the orders, Raul. You're just the watchdog. So be careful with that weapon. It…"

"Don't bait me, Antone."

"I would hate to have to turn in a bad report on you, Raul. Olaf is subject to such sudden anger."

The hand holding the Luger trembled.

Garson looked from one to the other, spoke through dry lips. "Look here! The American Consulate will know by eight o'clock tomorrow morning exactly where I am! If you two think you can…"

"How will they know?" demanded Raul.

"They'll…" Garson stopped, realized that he could be signing Villazana's death warrant. "I sent them a letter."

"The mail is not delivered at eight o'clock," said Luac.

"He's bluffing," said Raul Separdo.

"You expose your foolishness more and more," said Luac. "Garson spoke of the time with a certainty. He is merely concealing his messenger."

Separdo turned toward the house, still keeping his eyes and the gun trained on Garson. "Choco!"

Presently, they heard the outside door slam. Choco Medina appeared outside the screened enclosure, the pockmarks of his evil face like harsh black spots under the gas lantern's glare. He touched his mustache with a forefinger, nodded to Garson.

Garson glared at him. "You…"

"You know each other?" asked Separdo.

Luac spoke quickly. "I've had Choco keeping watch on Mr. Garson." He looked at Garson with an odd attitude of suspense.

Garson had the feeling that the situation had taken a peculiar turning.

Separdo looked from Luac to Garson. "Do you recognize Choco, Mr. Garson?"

"He looks like my Great Aunt Nellie on my mother's side!"

"What a calamity!"

"She was hung for treason!" said Garson.

"Every family has its secret shame," said Separdo. He raised his voice: "Choco! Come in and search Mr. Garson."

Medina entered the enclosure, came up behind Garson, bent over the chair and patted him with professional thoroughness.

"Where is the gun you were carrying earlier, Mr. Garson?"

"I lost it in the lake." He bit the words off, suppressing his anger, trying to see through the cross-purposes here. And abruptly he recalled Medina's warning at the car to conceal their relationship.

Could Medina still be with me?

"He's clean," said Medina.

52

"You have been watching him, Choco?"

"Yes."

"He says the American Consulate will know where he is by eight o'clock tomorrow morning. Do you have any idea how that could be?"

"Maybe he sent a telegram."

"Did you send a telegram, Mr. Garson?"

"Several of them."

"Why did you come here, Mr. Garson?"

"To find Antone Luac."

"Why?"

"I'm a writer. He's copy."

"What led you to believe you could find him?"

The threat of the Luger, the flat questions, the puzzle of this situation became too much for Garson. His anger boiled over.

"None of your damned business!"

Luac stiffened, put a hand on Separdo's gun arm. "Put away the weapon, Raul."

Separdo's eyes had lost their softness, had taken on a wild light.

Garson suddenly recalled El Grillo's comment on a man named Raul, and on Raul's anger.

"Put the gun away, I said!" repeated Luac.

"He will not talk to me that way!" said Separdo.

"Olaf will not like this when I tell him," said Luac.

Again the gun trembled.

"What led you to believe that Antone Luac was here?" asked Separdo. His eyes seemed to bore into Garson.

Luac said, "That would be the piece of manuscript Nita mentioned." He pressed down on Separdo's arm. "Now put away the gun."

Slowly, as though moving against pressure, Separdo lowered the gun, returned it to his belt.

"But where did he get the piece of manuscript?"

"Perhaps Eduardo," said Luac.

Separdo nodded. "Of course." He laughed, a brittle, chilling sound.

Garson swallowed, realized that he had been closer to death than ever before in his life, that Raul Separdo's symmetry of features concealed madness.

"We'll lock him in the end room under guard for now," said Luac.

"Perhaps in the morning we should let him swim back across the lake," said Separdo. He bent forward, staring at Garson, who was reminded of a jungle cat watching its prey.

"Take him, Choco," said Luac.

Medina touched Garson's shoulder. Garson arose, surprised at the trembling in his knees. He felt wrung out, without emotion. And his mind went back to Luac's words: *"Perhaps Eduardo." Eduardo Gomez?* Again he was touched by a sick premonition about the little Mexican.

Garson's prison was a square room of high ceiling, whitewashed beams. Tall windows looked out on the night. He could see light reflected from exterior bars. A heavy wooden bed jutted from the wall opposite the windows, a low nightstand on one side, a leather chair on the other side. Across the bed lay a red serape with a black eagle design worked in its center. A single yellow light dangling from a cord above the bed illuminated the room.

Raul Separdo followed them to the room, waited in the doorway. He stared from Garson to Medina with a look of questioning suspicion.

Medina crossed to a second door in the corner, opened it. "This is the bathroom," he said. And while his face was concealed from Separdo by the door, he winked.

Garson nodded, longed for a moment alone with the evil visaged Medina to unravel this mystery.

"That's enough, Choco," said Separdo. "Let's go."

They left the room. Garson heard the click of a key in the lock. He crossed to the dangling light, turned it off, checked the windows: heavy frames cemented into adobe. The bars outside looked even more secure. He crossed to the bathroom: no window, only a vent above the shower.

He paused, thought: *Am I trying to escape? Damn! Wild horses couldn't get me out of here before I've solved the mystery of this place!*

And he wondered then where they had secreted the queenly daughter, and if she knew of the hacienda's prisoner.

Garson slipped off his wet clothes in the dark, draped them across the chair and the foot of the bed. It was a soft bed, and he felt deep fatigue, but he could not sleep. He stared at the faint moonglow on the ceiling.

They don't dare kill me! But that Separdo's crazy! What game are Luac and Medina playing? Does Separdo have some hold on them? Who's this Olaf that Separdo fears?

He clasped his hands under his head, coughed, heard the cough echoed by someone outside his door.

Medina? Separdo? Medina would make himself known. He knows I'm popping with questions!

The warmth of the night was oppressive. Garson threw the serape off his bed. He recalled his agent's telegram.

Anita Peabody was involved with a Communist front. Does this really have something to do with the Reds?

Somehow, that idea didn't fit with Antone Luac's personality.

And where is Anita Peabody? There's something more here than a desire to remain hidden. Why would they think I'm with the secret service? What's Luac's secret—and why would they kill to keep it?

He saw the flare of a match through the crack beneath the door, again heard someone cough.

Garson stared at the ceiling, his thoughts clogged with questions.

The sleep of exhaustion overcame him. He slipped down into a dream peopled by a succession of Raul Separdos. The dream people appeared like stick figures parading past his eyes. A voice out of an echo box kept repeating: "To kill or not to kill? That is the question."

CHAPTER 4

arson awakened to the crystal chime call of a turtledove, heard a parakeet answer. He lifted his head, looked out the tall windows at the lake. A morning mist clouded the far shore. The lake appeared to be about a half mile wide. He could see the corner of a dock on this side, a boat chained to it, another dock directly across the lake.

He sat up, looked around his prison. The bed, chair and nightstand were the only furniture. His wristwatch on the nightstand showed 6:40 A.M. Garson picked it up, examined it to see if it had been damaged by the dunking. The watch appeared to be bearing out its waterproof guarantee. He strapped it to his wrist.

The door rattled, swung open. An ancient woman, skin almost black, hobbled into the room. She carried a tray containing a steaming pot of coffee, a tall glass of fruit juice, two fried eggs, beans and tortillas.

"The service in this jail is better than most," he said.

The old woman ignored him, placed the tray on the nightstand, turned.

"Do you speak English?" asked Garson.

She returned to the door, left the room without answering. He heard the lock click.

The food smelled delicious. He was surprised to find that he was ravenously hungry, pulled the tray onto his lap, began eating. The sun came over the hills beyond the lake, began burning away the mist.

Garson finished eating, found that his clothes had dried. He dressed, crossed to the barred window, stared out. To the right he could make out the barrio where he had waited in El Grillo's hut.

The daylight made the events of the previous day and night assume a sense of unreality. Garson wondered when he would see Luac's queenly daughter. He found this thought more absorbing than worry about himself or how he would escape from the hacienda with his story.

What had Villazana called her? *A mango.*

Garson smiled. He rubbed his chin, felt the stiff bristle of his beard, longed for a razor before encountering Anita Luac. There had been no shaving equipment in the room's bath.

Choco Medina opened the door at 7:45, put a hand to his lips, shook his head. "Good morning," he said.

Garson looked down the hall behind Medina, saw no one.

Again Medina shook his head.

Someone's listening.

"Is it a good morning?" asked Garson.

"Who knows?" said Medina. He stood aside, motioned for Garson to precede him down the hall. "Come on along."

The hall emerged into a large, cool room—high ceilings with hand-hewn beams that appeared smoke stained. The room's furniture was massive. Brightly colored rugs littered the floor, serapes on the walls. A fireplace in the far wall seemed designed as a base for the giant bull's head mounted above it. To Garson's left were low windows that opened out onto a terrace, a view of the lake and hills beyond.

Luac arose from a chair near the windows, leaned on his cane as he faced Garson. The remains of his breakfast were spread on a tray beside his chair.

"I trust you slept well?" said Luac.

"You're very trusting," said Garson.

Luac coughed. "You have rare insight." He nodded to Medina. "You may go now, Choco."

"*Sí, Patron.*" Medina returned to the hallway.

"So, our indomitable American journalist—fearlessly plunging onward against all odds—comes finally to the lion's den. It is just like the movies, Mr. Garson, no?"

"No." Garson sensed that they were playing a waiting game, talking for the benefit of someone else. He glanced around the room, saw no one else.

"Perhaps there is hope for you," said Luac. "Do you have a price?"

"It's a popular belief that everyone has a price."

The older man cocked his head to one side. "What's your price, Mr. Garson?"

"The story of your life!"

Luac's eyebrows raised, giving him the look of a quizzical demon. "Ahhhh! We are still in character. And what should I demand for this melodramatic price?"

Garson studied him. *Why this cat-and-mouse game? He wants something from me. That's obviously the only reason I was permitted to come here. Is he at cross purposes with this Raul Separdo? Am I supposed to take sides?*

He said, "You'll want me to keep your secret—where you and Mrs. Peabody are hiding."

Luac's face clouded, bringing sharp lines to his wide brow. "She is no longer with us."

"Oh. Where is she?"

"She is buried out there."

"What happened? Did something heavy drop on her?"

Luac's face darkened. He took several quick, short breaths, slowly regained control, spoke in a low, tight voice: "That is a course you should not pursue, young man."

"Sorry. I guess I let myself get carried away by the pleasant surroundings and pleasant company."

"You have received no more than a fool deserves!"

Garson nodded. "Whereas you are beset by unfair circumstances."

Surprisingly, Luac smiled, then chuckled. "You've spilled a bit of Mexican pepper on your tongue, eh? Well, this is no way to settle our difficulties. Now, if I permit you to do your story, how do I keep the tourists from climbing all over my hacienda?"

"You could mount a few tourists' heads on your fence posts."

"The thought has already occurred to me. Should I begin with yours?"

Garson stared at him. "What..."

"Enough!" Luac turned his head sharply, looked out the front windows.

Garson saw the old crone cross the terrace, go out of sight to their left around the building.

"We have only a moment," said Luac. "Please be quiet while I give you the essentials. You are in deadly danger from Raul Separdo, but I believe I will be able to hold him in check for awhile. We will try to help you escape. If you do get away, make no effort to help us. Just write your story about us. The publication..."

"But, what's..."

"We do not have much time, Mr. Garson. The old woman spies for Raul. Now, in my study, which Nita will show you later, you will see some manuscripts in a bookcase. Several have green bindings. One of those with a green binding had been torn slightly near the bottom. Take it out to read. Near the center of it you will find several pages that will help you do your story."

Garson nodded. His head was crowded with questions. He wondered if he'd have time to ask any of them. "Is Choco with you?"

"Yes. Trust him."

"What if I don't like the set up and just go away and forget you?"

Luac's eyes became slits. "Are we bargaining?"

"You mentioned prices."

"Do go on."

"I've nowhere to go."

Luac's glance darted to the hallway behind Garson. He raised his voice. "This has all been very pleasant, Mr. Garson, but I do not see how you could write your story and conceal our hiding place at the same time."

Someone is listening!

Garson coughed into his hand. "I could take a grand tour of Mexico, stop at many places. Ciudad Brockman would get lost in the itinerary."

"Bypassing several objections for the moment—how would you prove you'd found me?"

"In my luggage at the hotel is a small camera. It might also be possible for me to take back something you've written: an unpublished manuscript, perhaps."

Luac chuckled. "Ahhhh! The *price* goes up! A Luac manuscript might bring a small sum of money, eh?"

Garson felt the blood rush to his face. "Oh, no! I didn't…"

"Please!" Luac held up his right hand. "Don't spoil things just when I was beginning to gain respect for you." He dropped his hand to the cane. "Another question: What if some other enterprising journalist follows in your tracks and discovers that there is a Hacienda Cual near Ciudad Brockman?"

Garson frowned. "There's something I'd really like explained. Why such a simple anagram on your name?"

"My own monument to human blindness, sir—and because of the pun."

"What pun?"

"Cual. In Spanish it means *which*. The anagram becomes '*Which* Cual?' And the answer: 'The *Luac* Cual!' Very neat."

"Well, Mr. Luac, to answer your question: I plan to do such a complete story that there'll be no ground for another man to cover."

"Oh? And what of the idly curious—the human leaves that flutter on the wind?"

"We're back to the heads on the gateposts, I see."

"Yes. And you have such a distinctive head."

Garson swallowed. "What do you suggest?"

"Forget all about me for a sum of money—say one thousand dollars."

Playing to an unseen audience was beginning to tire on Garson. He shook his head. "No."

"How about two thousand?"

Again Garson shook his head.

"You name the price, Mr. Garson."

"Let's drop the subject for now, shall we?"

"As you wish. It may be bootless, anyway. Raul may want to keep you here as a pet."

Garson's interest rekindled. *Is Luac dropping a hint?* He said, "He wouldn't keep me here!"

"You have just made a foolish remark." Luac lifted his cane, tapped Garson's arm. "You don't know what we can do."

What's he trying to say? Garson wondered. He said, "You haven't seen my hand, either. By now, the American Consul knows where I am. They may get very stuffy about finding my head on a gatepost—or just finding me missing."

Luac nodded vigorously.

He approves of this turn in the conversation, thought Garson. He said, "I intend to do a story on you, Mr. Luac. One of the most important magazines in the United States is expecting it of me. I'd hate to disappoint them."

"Life has many disappointments, young man. Would you like to know what you're up against?"

Garson sensed the undercurrent of the conversation: *Information about our situation here.* He said, "It would help."

Luac gestured toward the lake with his cane. "The only roads out of here are across that lake. They are patrolled regularly by troops of vaqueros—our own cavalry." The cane came down, tapped the floor. "Behind us is a swamp in which a man can lose himself in five minutes—and die two hundred feet from safety."

"Very strategic," said Garson.

"The location of the hacienda? Yes. The good ones were always laid out like forts." Luac tugged at his goatee. "Then I have Choco. He was with Pancho Villa when he was eleven. His brother, you know, was one of Villa's lieutenants. I'm afraid Choco learned some very bad tricks with Villa."

The frustration of unanswered questions was almost too much for Garson. He sensed also that Luac was playing with him in some way—using him.

How do I get at the truth?

"Father!" Anita Luac's voice came from behind Garson. She came in from the hallway, her soft curves sheathed in a white sharkskin dress.

Garson felt his blood quicken.

She put an arm on the old man's shoulder, kissed his cheek, turned and looked squarely at Garson.

"I believe you two have already met," said Luac.

Her smile carried a hint of mockery. The large brown eyes seemed to say: "*I warned you!*"

"I have had the pleasure," said Garson. And again he wished that he could have shaved.

"You look just a little the worse for wear, Mr. Garson," she said. The warm contralto voice, too, carried the veil of mockery.

"Mr. Garson may be our guest for some time," said Luac. His voice sounded a shade reproachful, as though he reminded his daughter of something with the tone.

Her smile brightened. "It will be pleasant to have you here, Mr. Garson. It gets very lonely with just the same old faces."

Has she been told to play up to me? Why?

The old man leaned forward on his cane, glowered at the hallway behind Garson. "Choco?"

Garson turned. Raul Separdo came into view, moving softly on the balls of his feet. There was something suggestive of dancing in his motions. Garson found it easy to picture one of Separdo's ancestors dancing before a pagan idol while a priest tore out the heart of the sacrifice.

"Have we learned anything new?" asked Separdo. He bent his head to Anita Luac. "It's good to see you again, Nita."

Garson thought that her smile became a little strained. "You talk as though I'd been away, Raul."

"Every moment away from you is like a year."

Choco appeared in the arch of the hallway. "You called, *Patron*?" He swung a machete loosely in his left hand. The ends of his mustache drooped.

Separdo frowned.

"Yes, I called," said Luac. "You are to drop your other... work, and... uh... devote yourself to guiding Mr. Garson while he is our guest."

Separdo spoke without turning. "And if he attempts to escape, Choco, you may bring him back in pieces."

Anita Luac drew in a quick breath.

"He is not to be harmed," said Luac. "I hold you personally responsible."

Medina's right hand went to the revolver in his belt holster. "*Sí, Patron.*"

Separdo looked at the floor behind Luac, smiled. "I came to tell you that we have a message from the colonel of police in Ciudad Brockman."

Luac's goatee quivered. "Oh?" His tongue flicked over his thin lips. "What does my friend Bartolomé want?"

"He wishes to know if we have seen an American tourist named Hal Garson. Both the Consulate and Turismo have called him from Mexico City."

Garson stared at Luac. *Score one for me! Villazana did as he was told!*

"Ahhhh," said Luac. "Send the good colonel my regards, Raul. Tell him that Mr. Garson—an old friend—has kindly accepted our hospitality for an indefinite period, and that he would like his luggage sent up from the hotel."

Separdo nodded.

"You will recall my wise counsel of last night, Raul?" asked Luac.

"Yes, Antone."

"This is why Olaf still relies upon my judgment rather than yours, Raul. Olaf realizes that you are too—ahhh—quick."

Separdo scowled. The corners of his mouth trembled. Slowly, he smiled, turned to Anita Luac. "Are we going riding today, Nita?"

"Why..." She hesitated, glanced at her father.

"I'm sorry, Raul," said Luac. "Nita will be helping to guide Mr. Garson today."

Separdo's fingers curled stiffly like claws, then relaxed. "Of course. And Choco will be with them."

"Choco always guards my daughter, Raul."

"But naturally, Antone." Separdo looked out at the lake. "Such a beautiful lake," he murmured. "One never knows, does one? Beauty may conceal so many things."

Garson noted that Anita Luac was watching Separdo as a bird might watch a snake. Her hands were clenched into fists.

"As you say, Raul," said Luac. He turned to Garson. "Choco will loan you a razor if you wish to freshen up before looking around."

Medina lifted the machete in his hand. "Shall I loan him this one, *Patron?*"

Anita Luac laughed. It was like a release from hysteria. Garson realized that Medina's words had been aimed at just that effect.

"One of the little ones will do," said Luac. Laughter wrinkles deepened at the corners of his eyes.

Separdo nodded to Garson. "You must be careful that you do not cut yourself, Mr. Garson."

"Be sure you give the message correctly to the colonel of police," said Garson. "I wouldn't want him to worry about me."

"Worry is a bad thing," said Separdo. "No one must worry." He left the room, still with the lithe motions of a dancer.

Garson stared after Separdo. *What's his real function here? What hold does he have on Luac?*

"We will continue our discussion another time," said Luac.

"*Mañana?*" asked Garson.

Luac chuckled. "*Sí. Mañana.*"

CHAPTER 5

T his is my father's study," said Anita Luac. She opened a door off the hallway, preceded Garson into the room.

The noon sun beat down on the terrace beyond the room's front windows, reflected with a rippling glare off the white-washed ceiling.

Anita Luac crossed to the front windows, dropped bamboo screens across them, masking the view of the lake and sun scorched hills.

There was a hot mugginess in the room that Garson noted immediately as he entered. He wondered how Luac could work in that heat.

"Father uses this room at night," she said, as though answering his unspoken question. "He prefers the summer house in the garden during the day."

Garson nodded, looked around him. An intricate bird pattern in green had been worked into the golden tiles of the floor. A long trestle table stood parallel to the windows, its top littered with papers. A heavy rattan chair with a green velvet cushion had been pushed back from the table. The back wall of the room was entirely window-pane mirrors that reflected the masked view of lake and hills. Book cases floor to ceiling filled the side walls.

The green notebooks, thought Garson. He saw them on the right.

Medina followed them into the room, leaned against the doorway.

Garson moved idly across to the book case, studied the green-backed ones. He saw the marked one immediately, pulled it out.

"Your father suggested that I might like to read some of his work."

He flipped the notebook open to the title page: "The Duke of Pork." Garson frowned, thought, *I've seen that somewhere.* Below the title was written: "By George Merrill."

A pseudonym?

Then he recalled both author and title—*published within the current year in...* He could not remember the specific magazine.

Garson turned to Anita Luac. "Has all of this stuff been published?"

"Some of it. Many have never been submitted."

"Oh? Why does he write them?"

She shrugged. "He's a writer."

"Of course, but..."

"He calls the unpublished ones my insurance policy. If I ever need money—after he's gone..." Again she shrugged.

"You have only to submit this work by the famous Antone Luac." Garson nodded. "How does he submit the things he writes under a pseudonym? I mean: How does he conceal his identity? Does he have a friend working for him in the States?"

"Perhaps you should ask my father."

"I shall." He tucked the notebook under his arm.

She moved toward the door. "Shall we look at the rest of the house now?"

"Lead on."

They ended the tour at the dock that jutted into the lake beyond the front terrace. Garson stared thoughtfully across the water, noted from this new vantage point a large brick building down the lake to his left. Every door in the house had been opened for his inspection—almost as though he were buying property.

Just what am I supposed to buy here? he wondered.

Medina squatted by the lakeshore, rolled a cigarette, tipped his head back to protect his mustache as he touched match to tobacco.

Garson thought back to the room that had been pointed out as Raul Separdo's. There had been a desk without paper, a single chair, a bed made without a wrinkle. The room had felt unoccupied, as though Separdo had carefully kept every imprint of himself from showing there. Garson had the feeling that even Separdo's fingerprints were removed from that room daily. The effect was one of rigid concealment.

Concealment of what?

He focused on the building down the lake from them, pointed at it. "What's that building there—the one in the trees?"

Anita Luac moved up beside Garson, threw a pebble into the water. "That is another thing you must ask my father."

"Is that where they take the trucks?"

71

She stared at him silently.

Garson noted a total cessation of movement from Medina.

The tableau was broken by a call from behind them: "Nita!"

They turned. Raul Separdo walked toward them across the terrace, a cardboard box under one arm. His face appeared flushed, eyes glittering with an intentness that made Garson uncomfortable.

Separdo stopped in front of them, spoke to Anita Luac while keeping his attention on Garson: "Nita, your father wishes to see you."

"Right now?"

"Immediately."

She nodded to Garson. "If you'll excuse me?"

"Of course."

She crossed the terrace to the hacienda, went inside.

Separdo glanced down at Medina, who had not moved from his position beside the lake. "Why do you wait here, Choco?"

Medina flipped his cigarette butt into the lake, got to his feet, turned. "Because the *Patron* said to guard his guest."

"You may go with Nita."

"I'll wait. She doesn't need protection from her father."

Separdo's face darkened. The muscles at the corners of his mouth twitched. He turned to Garson. "Would you care to walk out to the end of the dock with me?"

Garson abruptly sensed menace like a thick fog in the air. He nodded toward the box under Separdo's arm. "What do you have there?"

"A surprise." The box emitted a scratching, bustling noise. "Come." Separdo took Garson's arm.

They walked to the end of the dock. The feeling of menace grew stronger with every step. Garson heard Medina's footsteps behind him. They stopped at the end of the dock. Garson glanced down at the rowboat there, noted that the chain was secured by a large padlock.

Separdo placed the cardboard box on the dock, slipped a hand under the lid and withdrew a young rooster. The bird squawked once. Separdo dangled it from one hand, appeared to notice Luac's green notebook under Garson's arm for the first time.

"What do you have there?"

"This?" Garson touched the notebook with his right hand. "Mr. Luac suggested that I might find some of his work useful to pass the time."

"Such time as there is," said Separdo. "Observe." He turned, flipped the rooster out into the lake.

It landed about ten feet from them in a splashing of wings, floated awkwardly for a moment. Abruptly, the bird was propelled half out of the water. Its wings beat frantically. It squawked twice: a quavering, agonizing sound. Then it went under. The water around it began to boil with hundreds of flashing forms. A slow red stain spread through the area.

"*Caribe*," murmured Separdo. He stared at the water with an intentness that frightened Garson, turned and looked directly into Garson's eyes. "They are called also piranha."

Garson swallowed in a dry throat, recalled his spill into the lake the night of his arrival. "I thought piranha were native to South America."

"These were stocked here especially to take care of meddlers," said Separdo. He stared at Garson with a gleeful intentness.

Medina stepped closer.

Garson felt the wild pulsing of his heart, the trembling of fear in his arms. *Is Separdo going to push me into the lake?*

"We will go back now," said Medina.

Separdo whirled on him. "Stay out of..."

"You've had your fun," said Medina.

"One day you will go too far, Choco!"

Medina's hand hovered above his gun butt. "One day the *Patron* will say to me, 'Choco, we have decided—Olaf and I— that Raul is no longer needed.' I will not play with you on that day, Raul. It will be quick!" He hooked his left thumb toward the shore. "Now, we go."

A violent shivering passed over Separdo. His lips twitched. The light in his eyes was like flame.

"See if you can beat me," murmured Medina.

Garson realized with a kind of awed remoteness that he was witnessing a scene that might have occurred fifty years before in the Old West: a trial of nerves. And he realized also that the evil-faced Choco Medina must be the only force on the hacienda keeping Separdo in check... with the exception of the mysterious Olaf. *Who is this Olaf?* he wondered. *What role does he play in all of this?*

Separdo's trembling subsided. He turned to Garson with a look of thinly suppressed violence. "I will go after I have said what I came to say: Mr. Garson, do not get any ideas about Nita Luac! She's not for you!" He turned, brushed past Medina, strode off the dock, crossed the terrace, entered the house.

"I thought I was going to have to take him that time," said Medina. He sighed. "I will be glad when we're off of this powder keg."

"What hold does Separdo have on Luac?" asked Garson.

"I'm sorry, Mr. Garson. It's not my place to give information."

"Thanks, anyway.'

"My pleasure."

"So Anita Luac is not for me."

"Nor is she for him," said Medina. "Shall we go?"

They moved toward the shore.

Anita Luac emerged from the house, joined them at the edge of the lake.

"Your father didn't want to see you at all," said Garson.

She glanced at him, frowned, looked at Medina. "Choco, what happened out there?"

Medina shrugged. "Raul fed the fish with a live chicken."

She shuddered. "That terrible man!"

Garson could feel a measure of calmness returning after his near panic. He said, "It was supposed to be an object lesson for me. Maybe I should be thankful. I didn't realize what *caribe* meant. I might have tried to escape by swimming the lake."

She took a deep breath. He could see her assume the mask of poise. "Do you dislike our company so much, Mr. Garson?"

"Call me Hal."

"When you've answered my question."

"Some of my companions are utterly charming," he said. "Others remind me that Spanish is a language with a special verb meaning 'to kill slowly.'"

"Spanish has many interesting verbs—Hal," she said.

Garson found that the nearness of danger gave him a new insight. There had seemed to be an invitation in her reply, but he recognized the effort that went into her pretense—and he still saw the light of mockery in her dark eyes.

"We must explore the Spanish verb forms some time," he said.

And he found himself regretting the pretense.

But a part of his mind was occupied with questions about the green notebook he carried under his arm.

What did Luac conceal here for me?

Garson excused himself to freshen up for lunch, went to his room.

The regular pages of the notebook were numbered. He found the inserted pages by riffling through the numbered corners until he came to three pages without numbers.

The first page was a family record for Anita Luac.

Her mother was referred to by maiden name: Anita Monser. The ancestry was traced into French Canada.

Antone Luac's record might have been copied out from a biographical encyclopedia. Garson recognized names and dates, out of his previous research.

Anita Luac's age worked out to twenty years. Her mother had been dead fifteen years.

The second page proved to be covered with rows of story titles. Beneath each title was a name, date and address. There were four names, among them George Merrill, the name attached to the story in the notebook.

Why addresses? Garson wondered. *Is there actually a George Merrill? Is Luac having people front for him rather than use pseudonyms?*

The back of this page carried another list of titles under the heading: "Unpubl. Luac."

Anita Luac's insurance policy?

The third page carried a brief history of Hacienda Cual—previous owners back to the period following the conquest, the list of improvements instituted by Luac.

On the bottom half of the page was a list of organizational names headed by "The Friends of The Poor," and beneath that another list of names. The list included one Olaf Sigurts, 21 Avenida Guzmán, Mexico, D.F.

Is that the mysterious Olaf?

Garson closed the notebook, stared at the cover.

What's Luac trying to tell me?

Choco Medina interrupted Garson's musing by bringing in the suitcase forwarded from the Palacio.

"This just arrived. Where'll I put it?"

"On the foot of the bed there." Garson got to his feet, tossed the green notebook onto the nightstand. "Choco, is Separdo a Communist agent?"

The reaction left Garson open-mouthed.

Medina threw the suitcase at the foot of the bed, darted to the door, peered down the hallway, shut the door, ran to the front windows, looked right and left. He was breathing heavily when he returned to plant himself in front of Garson.

"I don't think anybody heard you."

"What the dev…"

"I haven't had a fright like that since the night we took Parral. That's where I got this." He indicated a thin scar beside his nose. "Now, look, Mr. Garson—please think before you blat…"

"Is he?"

"Ask Antone Luac. Only, in the name of God, please do it when you're sure you're alone with him."

"What would've happened if I'd been heard?"

Medina lowered his voice. "The thing we're trying to avoid: a signal would've been given. Raul's boys would come swarming across the lake and…" He drew a hand across his throat.

"You've answered my question, Choco."

Medina frowned. "I guess I have."

Garson looked out at the lake. *So, in his own cute fashion, my ever-lovin' agent had it figured. But what did he have figured? What's going on here?*

"They'd come swarming across, eh?"

"Like locusts."

Garson shook his head. "One rifleman could hold them off. They wouldn't dare the *caribe*."

"After dark they would."

"Oh. Where does the Cricket stand in all this?"

"El Grillo?" Medina shrugged. "*Quién sabe?*"

Garson took the notebook from the nightstand, pulled out the inserted pages, handed them to Medina.

Medina glanced at them, swallowed, pulled nervously at his mustache. "Did Antone give you this?"

"Yes."

Medina looked at the doorway, then to the windows.

Garson said, "You'd better put them in a safe place. It wouldn't do for them to be found on me." He took a deep breath. "Now… can we talk?"

"No." Again Medina looked at the doorway. "It's time for *comida*—luncheon." He folded the papers, stuffed them under his shirt. "I'll carry these on me until you ask for them."

Garson looked at Medina's pock-marked face, thought: *Luac said he's to be trusted. But does Luac know? Maybe I've just made a serious mistake! And—good God! How do I know Luac's to be trusted? Maybe he wanted those pages to be found on me!*

CHAPTER 6

Luncheon was served for Luac, Anita and Garson in the summer house of the garden patio. The greenery around them gave an illusion of coolness, but there was no escaping the clinging heat of the tropical afternoon. Garson could feel the perspiration at his belt, the dampness of his neck and forehead. He wondered at the appearance of coolness maintained by Luac and daughter, decided that this, too, was illusion.

The crone who had delivered Garson's breakfast hovered over them, serving. She acted as a damper on conversation. Each time she bent over Luac, the old man fell silent.

Garson turned to Luac. "Who's the old woman?"

Luac wiped his goatee on a napkin. "Maria Gomez."

She stopped at the sound of her name, stared at Luac with an expression that made Garson think of a poisoner watching her victim. He suddenly lost his appetite, put down his fork.

"Does she speak English?"

Now, the crone looked at Garson.

"She understands what you're saying now," said Luac.

Garson felt uncomfortable, recalled that Luac had said the old woman was a spy for Raul Separdo. He looked up, met her eyes. They were like the eyes of a lizard with the lids down until only the thinnest of slits were exposed.

Luac seemed grimly amused. "Why'd you ask?"

Garson thought: *Because I saw that you're afraid of her! Because there are so many things I don't understand around here that I'll leap at any opportunity for information.*

He said, "Gomez. Are you related to Eduardo Gomez?"

"There's nobody by that name around here," said Luac.

But Garson was watching the old woman. She had seemed to crouch at the sound of the name. Her gaze darted to Luac.

"She's the sister of one of our men," said Anita Luac. "El Grillo—The Cricket."

"That's a curious nickname," said Garson.

"He was a sniper for Villa," said Luac. "It was said that he could hit a cricket in flight."

The old woman was still staring at Luac.

He motioned her to the kitchen with a curt movement of his hand.

The lizard gaze passed over Garson as she turned, shambled to the kitchen with a curious, leaning walk. It was though she moved her feet only to keep from falling forward.

Recalling her expression, Garson thought how he knew how the legends of the "evil eye" could have arisen.

"Garson, you would play with matches in a gas tank!" hissed Luac.

"Father!"

Garson was still seething about his discovery of Raul Separdo's role. *Shall I hit Luac with it now?* he wondered. But the old woman was returning with another dish of food. *Is Luac involved in some fantastic espionage plot?*

"A penny for your thoughts," said Anita Luac. She leaned toward Garson.

He tore his gaze away from the soft cleavage of her breasts. *Damn! Why's she playing up to me?*

He said, "I was thinking that your father's not the type."

"Type? For what?"

"For the role I have him cast in."

Luac lifted his chin, regarded Garson with an amused expression. "We didn't know you were casting."

"What role?" asked Anita Luac.

"Friend of the people," said Garson. He glanced at the crone, but she was intent on serving.

"You're right!" barked Luac. "I'm their enemy!" He chuckled. "You'll have to rewrite your script."

"I think I'll throw the whole thing away and start all over," said Garson.

This seemed to bother Luac. He coughed into his napkin.

Anita Luac looked concerned. "Are you all right, Father?"

"Of course I'm all right! Show Mr. Garson to his room, will you? And see that he's locked securely."

"I'm still under house arrest?" asked Garson.

"Let's call it protective custody," said Luac.

"Did Choco bring you your bag?" asked Anita Luac.

"Yes, thank you."

"There was a message with it from a Gabriél Villazana," said Luac. "He sent his kindest regards. We sent back word that you're having a happy visit here. Is that correct?"

"One never knows until the visit is over," said Garson.

"Spoken like a true disciple of Confucius," said Luac. "And a greater fool never lived. We will see you later, no doubt?"

"No doubt," said Garson. He looked up, caught the crone staring at him, her eyes open. The lids dropped immediately, and again there was the expression of the lizard in her seamed face. But for a moment, Garson had seen something: a dull look in the open eyes—something about her as though a terrible boot had crushed out her ego. And behind the dullness there had appeared a sense of watchful waiting.

Garson was struck by the sudden wondering thought: *Is she one of the meek who'll outwait us and inherit the earth?*

He followed Anita Luac to the door of his room, stopped there and looked down at her. "Let's stop this nonsense, shall we?"

She blushed. "What do you mean?"

"What's happened to Eduardo Gomez?"

"He was killed in an accident at Torleon." Her glance darted nervously up the hall. "It's so frightening! Maria is his mother." She looked back to Garson. "We think Raul told her that Eduardo was murdered..." She swallowed. "...and that Father ordered it!"

"What kind of accident?"

"I don't know. I didn't see the... I didn't see him."

"What made you decide to confide in me?"

She shook her head. "I don't know. It suddenly seemed like too much work to lie."

"Why's your father carrying on this pretense about Eduardo?"

"Because you asked in front of her. Things are supposed to be concealed from you."

"Does Raul want to marry you?"

"Raul?" She shuddered. "He has a wife and two children in Torleon."

"What's your father doing for the Reds?"

Her eyes became pools of fear. She put a hand to her mouth, shook her head. Presently, she whispered: "Please. You don't understand. If Raul..."

"I know! The cavalry would come galloping over the lake!" The heat of the afternoon, the unanswered questions, all were piling up on Garson. "You're all playing some stupid game, and you're trying to use me in it without telling me any more than you have to!"

Some of the mockery returned to her eyes. "You came for a story... Hal?"

He felt like pulling her to him, crushing her mouth with his.

She saw it in his eyes, stepped back. He could see her regain composure, feeling her control of the situation. "Sometimes one pays a price for a story," she murmured.

"What price are you paying?" he asked. "And for what?"

The questions shook her. "You're not amusing!" she hissed.

"I wasn't trying to be." He studied the lovely oval of her face. And he recalled Separdo's words: *Beauty may conceal so many things.*

Are there piranha in her soul? he wondered.

"Has Raul always been your watchdog?" asked Garson.

She shook her head. "Before him there was Maltzeff. Raul has only been with us for about eighteen months. Things were so different before. With Papa Maltzeff..." She sighed. "He kept a *casita*..." Her color deepened. "...a little house in town. Carmela—the woman—wasn't his wife, but they had nine children. We teased him that it was very Catholic of him." A hint of a smile touched her lips. "It used to make him angry. Religion, you know." She shrugged.

"What happened to him?"

"They called him home. Perhaps if we hadn't teased so much, he would've stayed." Again she sighed. "Poor Carmela."

"What does your father do?" asked Garson.

"You're trying to trick me!" She motioned to his room. "Please go inside."

"Okay, warden." Still he hesitated, looking down at her.

They heard Raul's voice in the room at the end of the hall.

"Hurry!" she whispered.

Garson slipped through the doorway, closed the door. He heard the lock click.

Trying to trick her? God, what a woman!

He crossed to the bed, stretched out on it with his hands under his head, tried to relax.

Okay, so I've learned something: Luac does some kind of work for the Reds. But what?

Garson could feel perspiration collecting at every place where he touched the bed.

This damned heat!

He got up, crossed to the bathroom, stripped off his clothes to take a shower. There was no window in the bath, only a vent above the shower stall. It was closed. He stood on tiptoes, opened the vent, froze in that position as he heard voices—very faint but distinct. One of them, he realized, was Raul.

"...without fail," said Raul. "Now hurry along with you." There came the sound of receding footsteps, then Raul's voice again, this time in Spanish: *"Sí? Que necesitas?"*

What do you want? Garson strained to hear the words.

A woman's voice answered, and he thought it was Maria Gomez. She spoke too rapidly for Garson to follow.

Separdo said, *"Ahorita no!"*

Not now! He sounded angry.

The woman's voice said, *"Sí,* Yegua." Her voice carried a tone of rebuke.

Then Garson began to tremble. *Yegua!* Slowly, he slid down from tiptoe, withdrew his hand from the vent. But he could still hear Separdo's angry voice telling the woman never to call him that—never!

Yegua!

He recalled the scene in the lobby of the Palacio, Medina telling about the murder of his brother.

Someone called "La Yegua." It must be coincidence. Choco said it was a common nickname for people of unpredictable anger.

Unpredictable anger!

Why was Separdo so angry at being called that?

Garson forgot about his shower, wrapped a towel around his waist, returned to the bed.

What do I do with this piece of information? Do I give it to Choco?

Somehow, this did not seem the correct move.

Garson was still debating the problem with himself after dinner that night when Anita Luac invited him to sit on the terrace "for the sunset."

She seemed filled with a gentle nostalgia, leaned back in a canvas chair, waved a hand at the horizon. "It would have all been mine."

Garson shifted his chair until he faced her. "What would? The world?"

"Don't be facetious!"

I suppose she means the hacienda, he thought. The curious tone of her words came home to him. *Would've been? What's to prevent it?*

"Where are you going?" he asked.

She looked at him out of the corners of her eyes. "Who knows?"

"Have you ever thought of marriage?"

"Once. He was the engineer who built our dam on the lower rancho. He had a wife and six children in Milwaukee. I was fourteen."

Garson smiled. "I have no wife and children."

She spoke without looking at him. "Is that a proposal?"

He felt a terrible distress close to the surface of consciousness, spoke in a low voice, "I believe it was. But I'd like to withdraw it and save it for a better time."

"And for a better woman?" He sensed tears in her voice.

"I didn't say that, Nita."

She made a visible effort to lift her spirits, straightened in the chair. "Of course you didn't. I'm sorry."

Silence came between them.

The brief tropic sunset swept its primary colors across the mountains, left them in the warm intimacy of the night. A full moon spread an iridescent carpet across the lake.

Choco Medina crossed in front of them at the lakeshore, outlined like a goblin against the moonpath.

Anita Luac arose from her chair. "I must be getting inside. The insects."

"And one particularly obnoxious bug called Garson." He got to his feet, faced her.

"I didn't say that."

"No. Of course you didn't."

"And you're sorry?"

"I'm sorry."

She held out her hand.

Garson heard Medina's footsteps on the terrace.

"Your guard approaches."

He took her hand, had the feeling that he should kiss it. Instead, he shook her hand in a short, hesitant gesture that made him feel silly.

Perhaps hand-kissing is more appropriate, he thought.

She slipped away into the darkness. He heard a door open, close.

Medina spoke at Garson's shoulder. "You like her a little, eh?"

"I do what's expected of me, Choco."

"Sometime you must try the unexpected. It works especially well with women." He lowered his voice: "Raul has been watching the two of you. It would be well to tread softly."

"Who really gives the orders around here, Choco?"

"You should not ask that question."

"Or I'll become fish food?"

"I am sorry to say that it has happened."

"Thanks for the warning."

"My pleasure." He motioned towards the hacienda. "I'll see you to your room."

Garson took a deep breath. *So many unanswered questions!* "And you'll see that the door's securely locked?"

"A door may be locked from either side."

At the door of Garson's room, Medina pointed to a newly installed bolt lock on the inside. "See what I mean?"

"Who's idea was that?"

"Mine."

Garson looked down the hallway, saw no one. *Should I tell him what I overheard through the vent?* The temptation was strong, but he let the moment pass, said, "Thanks for the thought."

"*Buenas noches*," said Medina.

"Good night, Choco."

A door may be locked from either side!

Garson threw the bolt when his door was closed, stared at it. *Try the unexpected? What did Choco mean by that? Does he want me to make a serious play for Nita Luac? And why shouldn't I? Maybe she's the weak link in this prison.*

In his bed after turning out the light, Garson chewed at his lower lip.

Could I get a message out to Villazana or the colonel of police? What about El Grillo? Choco said that El Grillo has a price.

But Luac said they would try to help me escape. Did he say that to lull my suspicions? To keep me from trying to escape? Why would he want me to escape and write the story that makes him out a traitor?

It doesn't jell! Damn! What's Luac doing? Writing? Writing what?

The reflection of the moonlight through his windows formed a pattern on the ceiling beams as of many crossroads— many choices.

What choices do I have? If I stay here and wait for them to help me escape—I could rot... or get myself killed by that crazy Raul Separdo!

Across the lake, a nightbird called, its shrill notes echoing like a cry of pain.

I've got to watch for my chance and get out of here, do it on my own. Nita's the weak link. Luac's using her to bait me. But two can play that game! God! I can't really let myself fall for that woman! I'd be finished for sure!

His eyelids became heavy, closed. Garson fell asleep with the image of the beamed ceiling still in his mind. It was an unsettled sleep, full of turning and searching, as though somewhere he had passed a crossroad and taken the wrong way.

CHAPTER 7

The door of Garson's room rattled, then it shook with a violence that brought him immediately awake. He sat upright in bed, looked out his front windows at the pearl grey dawn light on the lake.

Again the door was shaken and banged.

"Garson!" It was Raul Separdo's voice, high-pitched and with a note of frenzy.

Somewhere in the house, another door slammed. There came the sound of bare feet slapping heavily in the hall.

"What's all the commotion?" Medina's guttural voice.

"This door's locked from the inside!" snarled Separdo.

"Just a minute," said Garson. He got out of bed, slipped into shirt and pants.

"What do you want with Garson at this hour?" asked Medina.

"That is my business!"

Garson opened the door, saw Medina standing behind Separdo, barefoot and with his revolver in its holster belted over a ridiculous nightshirt.

Separdo was fully dressed.

Medina winked at Garson.

"What's all the fuss?" asked Garson.

Separdo pushed his way into the room, examined the bolt on the door. "Who put this here?"

"I did," said Medina.

"Why?"

"You just found out."

Separdo's lips twitched. He glared at Medina, turned the expression on Garson. "You were asking about the building at the lower end of the lake. I heard Nita telling Antone all about it!"

The sadistic light in Separdo's eyes made Garson think of the glassy eyes of a fish—of a *caribe*.

"So I was curious!"

"Is that why we're having this pleasant conversation so early in the morning?" asked Medina.

Again, Separdo's lips twitched. "That is one of the reasons—not that I'm required to answer the questions of a hired gunman!"

"Fashions in hired gunmen having changed so greatly since your application for membership was rejected," murmured Medina.

Separdo grinned. It was like the baring of an animal's teeth. "There's another matter I wish to discuss with Mr. Garson."

"You called the conference," said Garson.

"I saw you holding hands with Nita last night. If it happens again you will feed the fish!"

"Holding ha…"

"Antone's throwing you two together!" hissed Separdo. "He doesn't fool me. He thinks she's too good for me."

"Maybe he's just concerned about your wife and kiddies," said Medina.

"I have asked you not to interfere, Choco!"

"Several times, Raul."

"I was up before dawn today, Choco."

"Perhaps your conscience wouldn't let you sleep."

"I brought several of my men, Choco."

Medina stepped back into the hallway, dropped his hand to his gun butt. "I doubt that they can get me in their sights here."

"The whole day is ahead of us."

"Maybe it's not ahead of *you*, Raul!"

Separdo paled, stepped into the room away from Medina.

"Don't be a fool, Choco! This Garson is with the American secret service!"

Garson smiled wryly at Medina, took a deep breath. "How do you know I'm not with the Mexican secret service?"

The effect on Separdo was startling. He froze into rigid immobility, face ashen. Slowly, he turned, looked at Garson. The look was one of careful—fearful—measuring.

"How'd you know we haven't a dozen troops stationed around the hacienda right now—just waiting for my signal... or lack of it?" asked Garson.

Medina was smiling delightedly behind Separdo's back.

Separdo wet his lips with his tongue in a nervous darting movement. "Why... would... the... Mexican... secret... service... be... interested... in... me?"

"Maybe Olaf's tired of your bumbling," said Garson.

Separdo held his breath, mouth open, eyes staring.

Behind him, Medina's evil face registered absolute glee.

"Did Olaf send you to test me?" demanded Separdo.

Garson smiled, remained silent.

Separdo shook his head. "He wouldn't!"

"How long since you've sent patrols beyond the fences?" asked Garson.

Again Separdo shook his head. "But why would... But we have spies to tell... Did Olaf send you?"

"Why don't you ask Olaf?"

A weak smile touched Separdo's mouth. "Olaf knows I'm loyal! I do my best. I always do. I work night and day! I..."

"How long since you've sent patrols beyond the fences?"

"But Olaf never said..."

"Olaf shouldn't have to say!" Garson warmed to his role. The name "Olaf" was pure magic with Separdo. "If you were paying more attention to your work—instead of worrying about a female, you'd have thought out the possibilities."

Separdo swallowed, shrugged.

"Send those damned vaqueros back across the lake and get about the job that's expected of you!" said Garson.

Separdo stiffened, a look of suspicion entering his eyes. "Why should..."

"Now!" gritted Garson. "We had a hunch that you couldn't see anything else except Nita Luac!"

Separdo crumbled inside. He turned to Medina. "Did you know?"

"What do you think?" asked Medina.

Separdo's voice went up half an octave. "Did Antone know?"

"Same song, second verse," said Medina.

"While we stand around here whining about 'who knew' our perimeter is wide open!" snarled Garson.

Separdo nodded. "Immediately." He moved toward the
hallway, paused, turned, looked back at Garson with a puzzled
expression.

Garson frowned, glared at him.

Some of Separdo's self-assurance seemed to return. "Will
you be staying until after I've talked to Olaf?"

"That's the first sensible reaction you've had since I
arrived," said Garson.

Separdo smiled like a small boy who's been praised. "Olaf
knows I can do the job he…"

"When your mind's on the job," said Garson.

Separdo nodded. "Yes. But I still have questions about your
job, Mr. Garson." He turned, brushed past Medina, hurried
away down the hall.

Medina watched him go, turned to Garson. "Man, I think
we underestimated you!"

"What'll he do?" asked Garson.

"He'll contact Olaf immediately."

"And what'll Olaf tell him?"

"Olaf won't give him the time of day. That's the way he
operates: everything mysterious."

"Who is this Olaf?"

"A very powerful man, Mr. Garson."

"Come off it, Choco! Who *is* he?"

"Why don't you ask Antone?"

"I will. What'll Olaf do?"

"There's the rub." Medina frowned. "You acted correctly
here because it threw Raul into confusion. But we'll have to
move fast now. Olaf will go into action just as soon as he's
talked to Raul. And that, my friend, is not good."

"What're we going to do, Choco?"

"I won't know until I've talked to Antone."

"How long will we have?"

"It'll take Raul until tomorrow to contact Olaf."

"So long?"

"Maybe longer if Olaf is … away."

"Will Luac know?"

"Perhaps."

"Well, let's get busy!"

"Okay!" Medina saluted Garson. "Don't get carried away with your new success." He glanced down at his nightshirt. "I'll go get into some clothes and find Antone. Why don't you get some breakfast and meet us in the front room?" Medina turned away, trotted down the hall.

Garson slipped on a pair of shoes, went to the kitchen.

Maria Gomez was making tortillas, her hands patting the dough in steady rhythm. A blue haze of charcoal smoke filled the kitchen. Maria looked like an ancient witch bent over the coals. She heard Garson, looked up, watched him with the lizard stare while he crossed the room.

"Fry me a couple of eggs, please," said Garson.

"*Sí, Señor.*" She bobbed her head rapidly, moved with a quick subservience. There seemed to be a new fearfulness in her actions.

Has Raul been here ahead of me spreading the word?

"Hurry up about it!" growled Garson.

"*Sí, Señor!*" She moved dishes nervously beside the coals. One dish caught in her sleeve, crashed to the floor.

Maria glanced at Garson, bent quickly to clean up the mess.

"Who do you think killed Eduardo?" asked Garson.

The movement of her hands slowed, but still she did not look up.

"Answer me!" ordered Garson.

A pitiful shrug lifted the old shoulders.

I'm being a perfect beast! thought Garson. *But I have to act while I can.*

"What did Raul tell you about it?"

Now, she looked up at Garson, eyes wide open, only the dull waiting apparent in them. *"Por Dios, Señor!"*

Garson steeled himself against the pathos of her. "Do you know what will happen if you don't answer?"

"Sí, Señor." She arose slowly, shoulders bent, nodded her head. "Come now. I show." She turned, went out the rear door into the walled garden.

Garson followed her. *Now, what the devil?*

They crossed the garden by a dirt path. Leaves brushed Garson's face. A cobweb caught on his chin and neck. The path ended at a wooden gate in the brick wall. Pigs snuffled and grunted on the other side of the wall. The stink of a pigsty was heavy in the damp morning air.

Maria opened the gate. It creaked dismally.

They passed a line of concrete stalls, each with one pig. The animals set up an excited grunting, squealing and scrambling.

Now, the path struck directly into the swamp, became shadowy, smelling of rotten vegetation. A fetid, carrion odor wafted past Garson's nostrils. Insects leaped, buzzed and clung all around him, filled his hair, crawled under his collar.

The path ended at a fallen log. They traversed the log to another log, and yet another.

Where's she leading me?

Presently, a log lifted to a low hummock of moist earth thick with brush. He could see no trail. Maria plunged into the brush. Garson shrugged, followed. The brush opened to a narrow clearing atop the hummock, a fresh grave with a rude cross of limbs occupied the center.

Garson crossed to the grave. "Eduardo?"

Maria crouched beside the dark earth, bent her head. *"Mi hijo. Aieeeeee! Mi hijo!"*

My son!

Garson swallowed. *Why'd she bring me here? So we could talk privately? So I'd sympathize with her?*

"Do you know who I am, Maria?"

She nodded. *"Sí. Un hombre de Olaf."*

A man from Olaf. So Raul did spread the word!

"Did Raul say who killed your son?"

She arose, turned the lidded stare on Garson, spoke with a low, expressionless voice: *"El Patron! El hombre mas..."* Her voice broke.

Nita was right! Raul did try to pin it on her father!

Garson shook his head slowly from side to side. "No, Maria. It was Raul!"

"Raul?"

He nodded.

"Raul!" She raised her fists in front of her, opened her eyes wide.

"Cuidado!" said Garson. *Careful!*

And he thought: *What if I'm wrong? What if it really was El Patron Luac?*

Garson could almost see Eduardo's letter before his eyes: *"He kill mi!"*

I could have this whole thing turned completely end for end. Luac, his daughter and Choco could be playing me for the prize sucker of the century.

He said, "You must not let Raul know, Maria. You must wait. Do you understand?"

Her lids dropped. The lizard stare regarded him. "*Sí, Señor.*" She put a hand on his arm. "*Gracias.*"

He nodded, swallowed.

They returned to the garden. Maria left Garson by the wall, disappeared in the greenery to his left. He entered the garden alone, brushed through the heavy growth of plants, came to the rear door.

Raul Separdo stood in front of the door, his eyes narrowed, his manner one of careful waiting.

"Have you been for a walk in the swamp?" Separdo asked.

Garson noted dark mud on Separdo's shoes and trousers. *Did he follow us?*

"Why do you ask?"

Separdo pulled back his coat very slightly to reveal the butt of his Luger. "You understand, Mr. Garson, that if you have fooled me—if you are not from Olaf..." His teeth bared in a wolfish grin.

Garson suppressed his uneasiness, smiled.

"And about Nita Luac," said Separdo. "I would advise you..."

"I don't take your advice about Nita Luac. I don't take your advice about anything. Have you sent your men across the lake? And are you doing anything about the hacienda's perimeter?"

Separdo tensed, relaxed. "I will take this for now. As to my men—we have sent for the boat from the other side. I am going with them in a few minutes." He nodded. "I expect to find you here when I return."

"I'll leave when my job's finished," said Garson.

"Of course." Separdo turned, went around the house.

Garson watched Separdo leave, then went into the house.

Antone Luac was standing at the low front windows, watching Separdo and three men with rifles get into a large rowboat. A little runt of a man sat at the oars.

When Separdo also got into the boat, and they headed across the lake, Antone Luac grunted, turned, saw Garson.

"So kind of you to join us, Mr. Garson."

Anita Luac came in from the hallway wearing an open-necked green blouse, jodhpurs and riding boots. Medina followed her.

"Choco has told me of your inspired performance this morning," said Antone Luac. "I'm not sure *what* inspired you, but presumably it was the patron saint of all idiots!"

"Sorry you don't approve," said Garson.

"At this moment, Mr. Garson, I would almost enjoy watching you fed to the *caribe!*"

"What?"

"I had it all set!" snapped Luac. "You were to go riding across the lake there this morning and ..."

Anita Luac stepped forward. "Father, there's no sense going..."

"Raul just went across the lake with his men!" said Antone Luac. "You know what that means!"

Medina said, "I think we should try it anyway."

"What have I done?" asked Garson.

"Today, I had arranged for you to escape," said Luac. "And you—you descendant of an unbroken line of fatherless imbeciles! You've put Raul's entire guard force on the alert!"

"Father, he had no way of knowing," said Anita Luac.

Garson shrugged. "Maybe the imbecilic action was your failure to take me into your confidence."

Antone Luac snorted.

"Would you like to hear about my morning stroll with Maria Gomez to the grave of her son?" asked Garson.

Chins came up. They stared at him.

"Raul told her that you murdered Eduardo," said Garson. "She now knows that it was Raul himself who did it."

"Hmmmmph!" said Antone Luac. "Another needless complication."

"Sorry I interfered," said Garson. "You would no doubt prefer arsenic in your beans!"

"He's right," said Anita.

"He's a bumbling meddler!"

"Shall we go ahead with our original plan?" asked Medina.

"I don't like it," snapped Luac. "Raul could have his men knock off you and Garson, then…" he glanced at Anita.

"He won't dare move until he's contacted Olaf," she said.

Medina said, "And with Olaf gone…"

Antone Luac sighed. "I don't like it, but perhaps it's worth a try." He looked at Medina. "But, Choco, I want this understood: You're not to go ahead unless you make the contact with Pánfil and Roberto. Do you understand?"

"Naturally."

"And if *anything* looks strange to you, you are to call it off and return!"

"Yes."

Luac turned to his daughter. "If it's possible, I want you to go with them. Go straight to Tucson. You know who to contact."

"But, Father!"

"Do as I say," he snapped. "I can take care of myself."

"I will be here, *Señorita.*"

She frowned.

Garson looked from father to daughter, sensed the need they felt for each other, the unspoken bitterness of suppressed feelings.

"I will do what I think best at the moment," said Anita Luac. "And I will not argue more about it!"

Garson cleared his throat. "It would be a good idea to tell me what you're planning."

Antone Luac flicked a glance like a whiplash across Garson, looked at Medina. "Choco?"

"I agree." He looked across the room to the hallway. "Later, when I'm sure it's safe."

Luac returned his attention to Garson. "This time you will follow, please. I know it's difficult for one of your magnificent qualities, but…"

"I, too, will do what I think best at the moment," said Garson. He fought to conceal his anger. Felt like nothing would be more pleasant than to crash his fist into Luac's sneering face.

The old man sighed, glanced at Medina, shrugged. "Take food," he said. "It will be a long day whatever comes."

Once across the lake, they waited beside the dock while a peon saddled horses. Constraint about the presence of people walking on the trail above them held them in silence. They stared across the lake at the hacienda: a splash of tan and orange against the deep green of the swamp.

Abruptly, Anita Luac picked up a piece of wood from beside the dock—an axe chip about four inches long, three inches wide.

"Choco! Show me!" she shouted. It sounded like the ritual of a child's game. She hurled the chip into the air above the lake.

Medina's right hand blurred to his hip, came up with the revolver. There was a single shot. The chip bounced in the air. Another shot. Again the chip bounced. Five times he hit it.

The splintered chip fell to the lake. Something nudged it from beneath, then it was still.

Medina opened his gun, replaced the spent cartridges.

"The horses are ready," said Anita Luac.

"Now I understand why Raul was so hesitant," said Garson.

Medina grinned, flicked a finger along his mustache.

They rode out through a narrow trail in jungle growth that thinned as they climbed, opened onto a meadow. Smoky blue haze filled the air, hid the detail of the distant hills.

Anita Luac reined up in the center of the meadow, patted the neck of her brown gelding.

Garson stopped the sorrel mare they had given him, shifted uncomfortably in the saddle. It had been a long time since his last experience on horseback.

"The smoke," said Anita Luac. "The Indians are burning their *milpas*. They'll never learn!"

Medina galloped past them on a big bay, stopped, whirled, returned at a walk.

"*Milpas?*" asked Garson.

"Their cornfields. It's the way they clear them."

"This is a good place to talk," said Medina. "But keep your voice low."

Garson nodded.

"The idea is this," said Medina. "We are out on an inspection tour that will take most of the day. At noon we will stop for lunch..." he gestured to the bundle tied behind his saddle "...at a point about four miles from the Torleon-Ciudad Brockman highway. After lunch we will ride in that direction. Two men will be mending fences along the highway."

"This is the Pánfil and Roberto that Luac mentioned?"

"Yes. They are men we can trust. They will be in a light pickup truck."

"And we take the truck?"

"You and the *Señorita.*"

"What if we're followed?"

Medina patted his revolver. "The story is that you two are eloping. You will go to Ciudad Brockman where the colonel of police—who is another friend—will provide you with a car and driver to take you to the airport at Guadalajara."

Garson looked up at the smoke-dimmed hills, a feeling of premonition in his stomach. "Somehow, I don't like it."

Anita Luac's horse snorted, backed away.

"I don't either," she said. "But we'll give it a try."

Medina reached into his shirt pocket, brought out the papers from Luac's notebook. "Here. You'll want these."

Garson put the papers inside his own shirt.

Medina touched his reins. The big bay reared, turned, and they were off, racing across the meadow.

At noon they stopped where a narrow stream tumbled from rocks in a tree-marked watercourse. The air was cool with spray from the waterfall.

Medina tethered the horses while Garson and Anita Luac clambered down a clay bank to a sandbar beside the stream. Anita Luac waded across. Garson sat down on a log in the shade of the clay bank.

From the other side of the stream, Anita Luac called back: "Choco! Bring firewood. We can have tea."

Medina answered from above Garson. "*Sí, Señorita.*"

There came the sound of limbs breaking. A shower of dirt rained onto Garson. He looked up, saw part of the clay bank give way under Medina. The big Mexican fell on his side, began pulling himself upright with the aid of a vine. More earth caved from beneath his feet.

As Garson watched, the revolver slipped out of Medina's upended holster, slid down the clay bank. Garson picked it up, glanced across the stream at Anita Luac. She held a hand to her mouth, her eyes wide. He looked up at Medina on the clay bank. The Mexican had regained his feet. His pockmarked face carried a strange, set look, and he was staring across the stream to the bank above Anita Luac.

A horse whinnied behind Garson. He turned, still holding the revolver.

Raul Separdo sat astride a giant black stallion, outlined against the sky above Anita Luac. He held a rifle carelessly across the pommel, its muzzle pointing at Medina. Behind Separdo ranged three other riders, all carrying rifles.

They looked like nothing more than a raiding party of bandits. Separdo wore a black sombrero.

Separdo grinned. "What a pleasant surprise!"

Garson nodded.

Separdo looked at Medina. "*Buenas tardes*, Choco. I see that you have loaned your gun to Mr. Garson. What a pity! I would so enjoy another demonstration such as the one you gave at the lake this morning."

My God! He means to kill Choco!

Garson cocked the revolver. The sound broke loudly on the tense quiet.

"Ah!" said Separdo. "Perhaps Mr. Garson would like to give us a demonstration with the revolver?" He spoke over his shoulder to one of the riders. "*Pánfil! Un pedazo de madera, por favor!*"

A piece of wood! Then the name "Pánfil" registered. *Have we been betrayed?*

One of the riders dismounted, searched the ground, came up with a piece of wood.

"Show us how you can hit the piece of wood, Mr. Garson," said Separdo. "*Pánfil!*"

The man on the ground threw the wood into the air.

In that split second, knowing he could not hit the wood, Garson took a desperate gamble. He snapped a shot at Separdo. The Mexican's hat jerked from his head. His horse reared. He lost his grip on the rifle, which tipped forward, fell over the bank to Anita Luac's feet.

She snatched it up.

Garson stared at the confusion of milling horses on the streambank. *My God! I hit his hat!*

Separdo regained control of his mount, reined it up at the edge of the bank. His face was livid with fury.

Anita Luac stood beneath him, the rifle held at the ready. Separdo surveyed the scene.

"You do not like the small target?"

"I choose my own targets, Raul."

Separdo's hands tightened on the reins. "But Choco hit his target five times."

"I thought I might need the other four shots."

Separdo nodded. His lips trembled. "Did you hit what you aimed at, Mr. Garson?"

"Do you want to see another shot two inches lower?"

Separdo tensed, eyes wide, a wild light in them.

Behind Garson, Medina laughed. "Try him, Raul!"

Slowly, Separdo stilled his trembling. A smile like a nervous grimace touched his mouth and then vanished. "Perhaps we should continue on our separate ways."

"Perhaps that would be best," said Garson.

Separdo looked down at Anita Luac. "I will trouble you for the return of my rifle, Nita."

"I think I'll borrow it for the rest of the day," she said. "Maybe I'll find a target to my liking."

He stared at her, turned to the man standing behind him on the ground, then looked to another of the riders. "Jorge! Give Pánfil another drink."

Then Garson realized that the Mexican who had thrown the piece of wood was drunk, swaying, eyes glassy. One of the riders handed a bottle of tequila to the standing man.

"Tómelo!" snapped Separdo.

The man on the ground stared up at Separdo, lifted the bottle to his lips, drained it, threw the bottle to the creekbank.

"Pánfil was mending fences," said Separdo. "But we have other work for him today." He motioned for the man to remount his horse.

Pánfil staggered across to his horse, climbed aboard.

Separdo turned to Garson. "*Adiosito*, Mr. Garson."

Garson motioned with the revolver.

The four riders wheeled their horses, galloped away.

Medina slid down the clay bank to Garson's side, took back the revolver. Anita Luac splashed back across the stream, holding the rifle high.

"You were wise not to kill him," said Medina. He bent over the revolver, replacing the spent cartridge. "His men would've slaughtered us."

"What about your friend, Pánfil?"

"I suspect that his rifle was empty."

Anita Luac said, "You are a man of many surprises, Hal."

Medina holstered his revolver, looked at Anita Luac. "Has Pánfil betrayed us?"

"Never!"

"Then I..."

In the distance came the sound of a ragged volley of rifle shots, then the cold clear snap of the Luger.

"That bastard!" gritted Medina. "I'm sorry now you didn't aim two inches lower!"

"What was that?" asked Garson. But he felt that he knew.

"Pánfil," said Anita Luac.

"Did they kill him?"

She turned on Garson, her face suffused with rage. "Of course they killed him! The same way they killed poor Eduardo! The same way..." She broke off. Tears filled her eyes.

Garson turned, looked appraisingly at Medina. "Choco, did you know that Maria Gomez calls Raul 'La Yegua'?"

Medina stared into the distance. "I have suspected the connection for several days. How did you find out?"

Garson explained about the vent.

"Thank you, Mr. Garson," said Medina.

"For what?"

"For saving my life today... and for saving Raul for me. He's mine!"

"We'd better go straight back to the hacienda," said Anita Luac.

When they returned to the hacienda, Anita Luac stepped out of the boat, ran down the dock and across the terrace. Garson climbed to the dock, heard her calling for her father in the house.

Medina chained the boat to the dock, weighed the snap lock in his hand, hurled it into the lake, turned to Garson. "When I was with Villa, my brother loaned me for a time to be a batboy for an observer who came to us from Germany."

"Oh?"

"The observer's name was Rommel. He later became a famous general under Hitler."

Garson studied Medina's ugly face, wondering at the motive for this conversation. "Rommel of North Africa? The Desert Fox?"

"The same. Rommel was a colonel when I knew him. One day he said to me, he said, 'Chocito, to win a war is a very simple thing: You must be on the right side, and you must always be ready to surprise the enemy.'"

"To do the unexpected?"

Medina smiled, touched his mustache. "*Sí!*"

"What brought this up, Choco?"

"Today, you surprised the enemy twice."

"And he surprised us once."

Medina shook his head. "No. Nothing that swine does should surprise us! Nothing!"

"Am I also on the right side, Choco?"

Medina grinned. "That is for the Good Lord to decide, my friend. But I think you are."

Anita Luac and Garson ate dinner alone that night. The crone served them silently, avoiding Garson's eyes.

"Where are your father and Choco?" asked Garson.

"They are talking in his study."

"Has Raul returned?"

"No."

At the mention of Separdo's name, Maria Gomez looked at Garson. An evil smile touched the old woman's lips. She nodded once.

Would she poison him? wondered Garson. Then: *How much time have we? Has Raul contacted the mysterious Olaf yet?*

Garson finished eating, turned, stared out at the garden. He felt tense, uneasy.

Anita Luac put down her fork, got to her feet. "I would like to show you something."

Garson stood up, looked down at her. "What?"

She held out her hand, took Garson's. "Come."

They went out the front, around the house and along a sanded trail that sloped up to a low ridge looking down on the swamp and lake. Garson paused on the ridge, listening. He heard a truck motor laboring, looked down the lake to the mysterious building. It reminded him that he still did not know the basic secret of the hacienda: The role of Luac's occupation.

The afternoon sun cast long shadows across the lake, and the shadows hid the edges of the mysterious building.

What do they do there?

"This way," said Anita Luac. She tugged at Garson's hand. Her palm felt warm and trusting against his.

They went down the opposite side of the ridge into a garden grove of eucalyptus trees. Two rock-bordered graves with stone crosses occupied the far side of the grove.

My day for visiting graves!

"I have a feeling I will never see this place again," said Anita Luac. She stopped beside the graves. "My mother and my brother. He died when I was very small. Fever." She disengaged her hand, sat down on the grass beside the grave, spread her skirt. "I used to play here when I was little. This was a separate pretend world all my own."

Garson had a sudden mental picture of a doe-eyed girl— like an enchanted naiad—playing in the grove by the lake. The thought filled him with sadness.

Bats began swooping about them in the warm evening air.

"Why did you bring me here?" he asked.

She looked up at him, shrugged. "It was a whim."

"You must have been a lonely child."

She got to her feet, brushed her skirt. "Yes. But I didn't realize it at the time." She smiled. "I had the ghosts here. Do you believe in ghosts?"

"I don't know what to believe about ghosts."

"I've never made any big decision of my life without consulting these ghosts."

"Did you come here this time to make a decision?"

Again she shrugged, kept her face averted.

Garson moved closer. She drew away. He followed, touched her shoulder. She turned, stared up at him, a look of total absorption in her large eyes, as though she drew into them everything that she saw.

With a fierce possessiveness, Garson pulled her to him, bent his mouth to hers. She seemed passive at first, then a fluttery response awakened her. The kiss became something explosive, demanding. He was totally aware of every place where their bodies touched. Her left hand went behind his neck. She moved her head softly from side to side, never breaking the kiss.

He dropped his right hand to her waist, bent her back. She yielded, then stiffened. Slowly, she pushed him away, stood before him, breathing rapidly, one hand at her throat.

Garson regained self-control as though it seeped upward from his toes. His breathing slowed, and he became conscious of the look in her eyes, the light of mockery.

"No man ever kissed me like that before," she said.

He swallowed. "How did it make you feel?"

She drew in a deep breath, shook her head without removing her attention from his face. "It filled me with... with a sense of power!"

She's making a fool of me! he thought. *They're using me! And she's the bait!*

"Power over me?"

"No. Power over life."

God help me! I don't care if I'm being used!

He reached for her, but she pulled away.

And he thought: *How would a man like Luac train his daughter? To take and never to give!*

Swift tropic darkness settled across the grove.

"Shall we be getting back?" she asked.

The moon sent a faint, ghostly light through the trees. Garson tried to see her face by the glowing, failed. She was a shadow against shadows.

"We should have thought of that earlier," he said.

"Sorry you came?" She sounded lightly unconcerned.

"Always glad to further my education," he said.

Garson left her at the rear door of the house, sat down on the rough wood bench beside the door. His leg and thigh muscles were beginning to complain after the day on horseback. There was a dull ache behind his eyes that the soggy warmth of the night did nothing to ease.

For the first time, he began to review the day. It left him with a sense of shaking horror. And the mysterious Olaf loomed over it all like the sinister embodiment of everything evil that could be seen in Raul Separdo.

What are Luac and Medina planning? Why don't they draw me into their conference?

My God! Why did I have to let myself fall for that woman?

The door beside him opened, closed. Choco Medina joined him on the bench.

"Why is the *Señorita* crying?" he asked.

Crying?

"I don't know, Choco. Maybe she's afraid. The Lord knows I certainly am."

"Where did you go on your walk?"

"A grove of trees over there. The graves of her mother and brother."

"Ahh. Perhaps that is it." Medina nodded. "I came out to tell you how the situation stands."

"Black?"

"Very black, but perhaps not hopeless."

"I knew it when Separdo rode up on us that way."

"There are some things in our favor. For one, Olaf is in Guatemala. He will not return for several days. For another, Raul sent word to Maria Gomez that she should dope our food tonight to make us sleep."

"What's he planning?"

"I think he is planning to come across the lake by night and take over control of the hacienda with his men, but thanks to you we are warned."

"Thanks to me?"

"Maria came to us as soon as she received the message. She wants revenge on Raul."

"I don't understand that, Choco. All I had to do was tell her it was Raul who killed her son—and she believed me."

"She has been with the Luacs for sixteen years, my friend. She needed only to have someone tell her what her instincts already knew."

"Why didn't he just take us today, Choco?"

"Raul? I've been trying to answer that question. I think it was because the *Señorita* had the rifle. He knew he'd have to kill her to take it, and he does not want to do that."

"He's a fiend!"

"The truth. It is also in the nature of this fiend to toy with his victims. He likes to strike fear into the heart. And

Frank Herbert

today he had poor Pánfil to demonstrate his power of life and death."

"God! How'd Luac ever get into his power?"

"He had no choice. One day there was Raul—the new watchdog."

"What're we going to do tonight, Choco?"

"We have a dozen flares. The moon will give us light for many hours. After that we will use the flares. They cannot cross the lake while we have light to shoot."

"The door has a lock on both sides, eh?"

Medina chuckled. "*Sí*, and the *caribe* in the middle."

"You'd better give me a gun, Choco."

"Or course. But please do not lose this one in the lake."

Garson recalled hiding the other revolver under the log. He told Choco Medina about it.

"You are very wasteful of good firearms, my friend. That one will be useless with rust by this time. But I will go get it tonight." He put a hand on Garson's shoulder. "The *Señorita* likes you."

"Oh?"

Medina squeezed Garson's shoulder. "I would die for the *Señorita*, my friend."

Garson felt a choking sensation in his throat. "God help me, so would I!" he whispered.

"I suspected that you had hidden the gun," said Medina. "But now I know that you trust me. I want you to know that I have trust for you—and after today, a special trust in your gun hand."

Should I tell him the truth about that? wondered Garson. *That I was aiming to kill Separdo, and missed by the grace of God?*

115

Medina got to his feet. "I must join Antone. We will be in the front room."

He entered the house, closing the door softly.

Garson stared into the darkness. *How long can we hold out? Separdo has an army across the lake.*

Something stirred the leaves in the garden. A twig broke under someone's foot. Garson tensed.

Anita Luac came into the faint moonglow of the open area beside the door. "I listened to you and Choco," she said.

"How long can we hold out?" he asked.

"This place is a fortress," she said.

"What's your theory on why Raul held off today?"

"He's afraid you're really from Olaf."

"Given time, any fortress can be taken, Nita."

She moved closer. "Is that your theory about women?" The faint mocking glint in her eyes was very clear to him.

Garson had the feeling of being outmaneuvered, trapped. *This is what the old man wants! He wants me to be her slave and thus his slave! Why? What can I do for them?*

"What are you thinking?" she asked. "You look so withdrawn."

"Maybe I was trying to retreat."

"Are all of your defenses gone?" She slipped her arms around his neck, pressed herself against him, lifted her lips.

Garson stared down into the brown wells of her eyes. They seemed to draw him down... down... down until their lips met. He felt himself melting with desire.

She broke away with a violent push against his shoulders, stepped back.

Bitterness overwhelmed Garson. "Testing your power again?"

She drew in a shaky breath, spoke in a faint voice. "My willpower."

He took her hands, felt them tremble. "Why were you crying?"

"Perhaps you reminded me of how lonely I've been."

"Nita, do you care for me at all?" The question came out as though torn from him.

She jerked her hands free, whirled away. "Why should I care for you? Because you've kissed me?"

He started to put his hands on her shoulders, drew them back. *A slave! Begging for favors! Luac knows his man. Here's the price I can't refuse.*

The bitterness filled his voice. "Maybe you should care for me because that's what your father has instructed you to do!"

She whirled, slapped his face. He staggered backward.

"You're a beast!" she hissed.

"That's right! A beast in love with you!" He grabbed her arms, pinioned them, crushed her mouth beneath his. She bit his lip, kicked at him in blind fury, then relaxed against him, sobbing.

He stroked her hair. "I'm sorry, Nita."

"No. You have every right to hate me. Please hate me!" She pushed away, ran from him. He heard a door slam.

That ties it!

Garson stormed into the house, down the hall to the front room. Luac and Medina stood by the windows, staring at the moonglow on the lake.

"All right, Luac!" barked Garson. "I want answers!"

Luac turned slowly. "Ahhh. Young Lochinvar!"

"You're asking me to get myself killed!" said Garson. "For what?"

"Steady," murmured Medina.

"For what?" demanded Garson.

"Perhaps for the story you were so anxious to get."

"You've never had any intention of letting me do that story!"

"Now there you're wrong."

Garson was startled into silence. There had been something flatly convincing about Luac's quiet reply.

"Why else would I want you to escape?" asked Luac.

"I have only your word for it that you wanted me to escape! The whole thing could've been a put up job!"

"Including Raul Separdo?"

Again Garson fell silent. *I'm caught in the oldest trap in the world: a prison of my own building! Some of the things that've happened I know are real—not make believe.*

He studied Luac in the moonlight: dignity and a kind of cynical amusement. The old man began humming, stopped. "Do you know that song, Mr. Garson?"

"Why should I?" His voice revealed his resentment and frustration.

"Because that song is Mexico. *Cuatro Caminos!* Four roads. There are four roads in a man's life. Which of the four is best?"

"You're talking nonsense!"

"Oh, no! For each road there is a different price."

"Have you offered me the price I can't refuse? What's down that road?"

"That is the big joke, my friend. There is only one thing down all of the roads: death! You merely arrive at it by different routes."

"You haven't answered my question, Luac."

"About price? Your question was not clear."

"Are you offering your daughter?"

"You are a fool!"

"Oh, am I?"

"My daughter makes her own offers."

"And decisions?"

"Naturally!"

"Can she make the decision to leave here with me tonight?"

A bitter laugh shook the old man. "And how do you propose leaving? By flying out on the wings of love?"

"Maybe I'll just go over and get Raul Separdo's permission!"

"Hah!"

"Fighting among ourselves will not help us now," murmured Medina.

"What about the swamp?" asked Garson.

Medina shook his head. "There's no escape that way."

Garson stared at him in the gloom. "Choco! What about El Grillo?"

"What about him?" asked Luac.

"How do you signal him to come for you?"

"Don't be an utter ass! He thinks I killed Eduardo!"

"All right, Luac! What's *your* plan?"

"Choco will try to get out tonight by working along the edge of the lake in the swamp."

"I think it can be done," said Medina.

"And what if he does get away?"

"Although it is a very poor solution and will create a situation that will be very bad for me, he will bring the *Guardia Civil*," said Luac.

"Why will it be bad for you, Luac?"

"I choose not to answer. If he succeeds, you will learn the answer. If he fails, it will make no difference."

"I think you're both being damned stupid," said Garson. "A whole armada of canoes could work along the shore on both sides of the peninsula and take us by force."

"That is what they will try," said Luac. "But they reckon without this." He motioned to something on the shadowy floor beside him.

Garson moved closer, peering at it.

"A Lewis gun," said Luac. "Even Raul didn't know about it! We buried it beneath the files of my study."

"A little memento from the revolution," said Medina.

Garson stared at Luac. *He hasn't answered a damned one of my questions!* He said," You're a bunch of…"

Anita Luac's perfume wafted past his nostrils.

Her voice came from the darkness behind him. "We're a bunch of what darling?"

She came up beside him, slipped her arm beneath his. For all that her actions betrayed it, the scene in the garden might never have happened.

"Maybe you'll tell me, Nita," said Garson.

"Tell you what?"

"What's the connection between your father and Raul Separdo?"

She looked at the shadowy figure of her father. "Has he refused to tell you?"

"You know he has!"

"*Paz y pan,*" murmured Anita Luac.

"Nita!" her father snapped.

"I make my own decisions, Father, remember?"

Luac snorted.

"*Paz y pan*," she repeated. "Peace and bread."

Garson recalled seeing the slogan stenciled across a hammer and sickle design on the mud walls of a slum quarter in Guadalajara.

"But now it's death and blood!" she said.

"What's the communist slogan have to do with this?" asked Garson.

"My beloved father's supposed to be one of their head propaganda writers for the Western Hemisphere."

Luac turned away from them, stared out at the lake.

Garson absorbed this thought for a moment. He still could not fit the idea to Luac's personality. "Supposed to be?" he asked. "Is he or isn't he?"

"Oh, I think he was once. And he trained others, too. We had a regular school. But that was before mother died."

"You're handling this very badly, Nita!" barked Luac.

"But I'm doing it my own way, Father."

"A propaganda school," prompted Garson.

"My father's so very clever," she whispered. "His stories are always published. And then they carry subtle little twists for the American market: a sympathetic Russian here—a little race prejudice there—a dirty capitalist or two—a brutal American soldier—an atrocity story with a Yankee setting—stories to make the U.S. Government look bumbling and stupid."

"I've read them."

"Millions of people have, Mr. Garson." She sighed. "The organization is very far reaching. We have agents in the U.S. who send the stories as their own—write a few themselves."

Garson felt the paper under his shirt, recalled the list of names and addresses.

"What's he really doing?"

"I'm not really sure. He says that the surest way to expose a sham and stupidity is to do a caricature of it. He says that fools like Raul can't understand this."

"But Olaf does!" snapped Luac. "That's really why we're in this mess." He sounded petulantly defensive.

"Nita is explaining this," said Garson.

Luac snorted.

She said, "He means, I believe, that if you *over*make a point—lay it on too thickly—then people see through to the weaknesses."

"Oh. So he's really been a double agent—working secretly against his masters."

"That's what he says."

"Are you quite finished, Nita?" asked Luac.

"No, I don't believe I am, Father."

"Was your mother a communist?" asked Garson.

"Leave her out of this!" barked Luac.

"Yes, she was a communist," said Anita Luac.

Garson felt the dryness of his mouth, swallowed. "And what're you?"

"I'm my father's little joke on our jailers. He taught me to hate them."

"You're a secret salesman for democracy."

"Hah!" said Luac.

"How did they keep you in this jail?"

"We were never permitted off the hacienda together. Always one as hostage for the other."

"What do the trucks bring?"

"Paper. The mysterious building is a printing plant. They print pamphlets for distribution all over Latin America."

"Are any of the people across the lake loyal to your father?"

"A few of them. But they're afraid of Raul. You saw what happened to poor Pánfil."

Garson looked at the dark figure of Medina in the shadows by the windows. "What about you, Choco?"

"What do you mean?" He spoke without turning.

"How do you fit into all this?"

"Oh, the *Patron* and I have been together for years."

"Father saved Choco's life during the revolution," said Anita Luac.

"Why hasn't Raul just forced his hand with you, Nita?"

"Because he had to answer to Olaf for what father writes."

"And Raul is afraid of Olaf. One more question: Who's Olaf?"

"Latin American director for the Communist International. He was mother's half-brother."

Garson looked at Luac's back. "You know, Luac. It appears to me that you let your emotions trap you just as securely as I did."

"Hah!"

"Stalemate," said Garson.

Anita Luac said, "I believe I've told him the essentials, Father."

Luac turned, looked to Garson. "Which only proves that one's own blood is not immune from idiocy!"

"Perhaps an immunity like that is passed down from the parents," said Garson.

"Idiocy compounds idiocy," said Luac. "And there you have the history of the world."

"I still find it hard to believe you're a communist."

"There may be hope for you yet, Mr. Garson. I could answer the famous congressional question with all honesty: I am not now, nor have I ever been a communist."

"You've been writing their propaganda."

Antone Luac chuckled. "My little joke."

"I'm hysterical!"

"Hah! Democracy! A legion of fools pushing each other over the edge of nowhere. Good government died with the absolute monarchs."

"Long live King Luac!"

"The government of the United States has a few saving graces," said Luac. "Vestiges of aristocracy. They're moving away from it, though, toward..."

"Toward your pals in Red?"

"As a matter of fact, yes. And there we have the ultimate idiocy: the gigantic conglomeration of fools—asses—in full control of their own short destiny. That's my capsule definition of communism."

"But you've been helping the..."

"The world of fools is demanding this change, Mr. Garson. I think it is the greatest cosmic joke possible to give them a little peek into their own demise! And the really choice part of the joke is this: All the time I'm pushing, I am telling them precisely what's wrong with the prison!"

A silent laugh shook him.

"For this you put yourself and your daughter into... into..." Garson waved a hand around him.

"There were other considerations at the time. Anita's mother played the game seriously. Communism was a toy to her: a wonderful diversion. It pleased me to let her play with her toy."

Anita Luac said, "Father, stop it!"

"No, my dear. When you opened the conversation with our young friend here, you made my present comments inevitable. When one pulls the stopper out of the tub, one cannot merely wish the water back into it."

Garson said, "But you're trapped here!"

"Oh, quite."

"A blind moron would've seen that this situation would become impossible."

"I was a blind moron."

"You know what'll happen to Nita if Raul takes her!"

"He won't take her... alive."

"*Patron!*" said Medina. "They are assembling canoes and boats along the opposite shore." Luac turned away from Garson, bent over the Lewis gun, pushed it forward into a patch of moonlight. The fins of the machine gun's air-cooled barrel cast weird shadows on the floor.

"Smash the window there to give me a better traverse," said Luac.

Medina took up a rifle, swung it by the barrel to shatter the glass.

Garson crossed to Medina's side, found a row of rifles across the arms of a chair, took one.

"Don't fire until the order is given," said Luac. "Choco! Give us a little light."

Medina fumbled on the seat of the chair, crossed to the door, opened it, stood in the protection of the wall while he aimed something out across the lake.

A rocket arched from his hand, exploded into brilliance above the lake, drifted down slowly swinging from its tiny parachute.

In the sudden light, they could see masses of canoes and a scattering of rowboats along the far shore. Men ran from them, scrambled into the shadows of the trees.

"Shall I sink their navy?" asked Luac.

"It would be a better object lesson to wait until…"

A rifle bullet splatted into the door beside Medina. He dropped to his knees.

"That came from this side of the lake!"

"Where?" asked Luac.

"The little ridge up there above the graves."

"Are the doors all locked in back?" asked Luac.

"*Sí!*"

"Where's Maria?"

"*Aqui, Patron!*" The old woman's voice came from the darkness behind them.

"Get down!" ordered Luac. "They will be shooting from the other side in a moment."

Medina slipped away from the door, padded away into the darkness at the rear of the house. Presently, he returned. "All bolted down tight. We'd hear anyone before they could get in."

Garson was staring to the right, down the lake toward El Grillo's barrio. In the glare of the flare he could see the entire curve of shoreline. He looked to the left, saw that the ridge hid a short piece of the shore.

"They will come from the left," said Garson. "They will try to get into the protection of the ridge, come up the other side until they can infiltrate the whole area."

"He's right," said Medina. "I believe I'll go out and discourage them as soon as the flare dies."

"Antone!" It was a long, hallooing call from the ridge.

"Raul!" said Luac. "Don't answer him!"

"We know you're in there, Antone! Come out with your hands up."

The flare sizzled to darkness in the lake.

Medina slipped out the door, faded into the darkness.

"Come out with your hands in the air!" called Separdo.

Luac said, "I feel something in the wind. I will give odds that Olaf has arrived."

Garson felt a shudder pass over his body, jumped as Anita Luac brushed against his arm, lifted one of the rifles from the chair.

"A one-man picket line!" snapped Garson.

"Ahhh, but he was with Villa," said Luac.

"And I was with the Marines. This situation stinks!"

"What do you suggest, Mr. Garson?"

"Is there a chance that El Grillo will help us?"

Luac turned his head slightly without taking his attention from the lake. "Maria? What about that? He's your brother."

"Quien sabe, Patron?"

"Send Maria for El Grillo," said Garson. "Maybe in the confusion, we could…"

"El Grillo is also Raul's cousin," said Luac. "We cannot be sure of him. And there's another complication." He hesitated.

Garson crept up beside Luac. "Yes?"

"Eduardo was a favorite with El Grillo. What's your guess on the story Raul gave him?"

"We've got to find out," said Garson. "Raul doesn't know yet that Maria's with us."

"But he suspects," said Luac. "Otherwise, he'd have just walked in, believing all of us in a drugged slumber."

Maria's feet slithered up behind them. She spoke in a heavy accent: "Meester Garson?"

"Yes?"

"Why deed Raul keel my sahn?"

"Because Raul found out that your son brought Mr. Garson here to spy on him," said Luac.

"I weel go," she said.

"It's very dangerous," said Luac.

"*Sí. Entiendo, Patron.*"

I understand. The words were spoken very softly and simply.

"Well, I'm not ordering her out there," said Luac. "I refuse to participate in any more idiocy!"

A fusillade of rifle shots rang out along the ridge. Immediately, several probing bullets splatted against the thick adobe of the front walls—all fired from across the lake.

"Stay down low!" hissed Luac. "Nita?"

"I'm all right, Father." Her voice sounded calm, as though she had come to some understanding with herself.

Presently, Medina scrambled through the front door.

"I could see you coming down most of the way," said Luac. "Why didn't they shoot at you?"

"Perhaps because they have retreated back off the ridge and into the grove," panted Medina. "I am hit in the shoulder. It is just a scratch, but I would appreciate a bandage."

"What's it like out there?" asked Garson.

"It is very open, my friend. There is not much cover on this side of the ridge. I went clear back to the swamp before moving up."

Anita Luac came up beside Medina, moved him into a patch of moonlight. "I got the first-aid kit."

"Did you get any of them?" asked Luac.

"One, but I do not think it was Raul."

"How many are there?" asked Garson.

"There is only one canoe on the…" He drew in a sharp breath, *"Aieee! Madre de Dios!"*

"I'm sorry, Choco," said Anita Luac. "It's the only disinfectant we have."

"Puro fuego!" he said. *Pure fire!*

She tied a bandage around his upper arm. "I can't see very well, Choco, but it looks like a clean wound just along the edge of the bone and through the muscle. The bullet went right on through."

"I have cured such as this with nothing more than a good night's sleep," said Medina.

"You're not going to get that sleep tonight," said Garson.

Medina chuckled. *"Sí.* I will stay awake."

Maria Gomez moved to the door. *"Choco! La luz!"* she said. *The light!*

"What's going on?" asked Medina.

"Mr. Garson had the brilliant idea to send Maria for El Grillo."

"What could *he* do?"

Garson said, "He could come to that mudbank on the right over there where he brought me the first night. He could do it as soon as the moon is down."

"As soon as the moon is down, that lake will be swarming with canoes," said Medina.

"We could discourage the first swarm with a flare and the Lewis gun," said Garson.

"And likely discourage El Grillo in the bargain!" snapped Luac.

"Not if Maria explains this to him."

"I explain," said Maria Gomez.

"This is a mistake," said Luac.

"*Porque la luz?*" asked Medina. *Why the light?*

"So they see me."

"They'll think she's escaping," said Garson.

"She'll be a nice clear target," said Luac.

"Maybe you shoot at me, too," she said.

"No!" snapped Garson. "They know we wouldn't shoot at you. If we did shoot, they know we couldn't miss. It'd give the whole show away."

"*La luz, Choco,*" she said.

"What about it, *Patron?*" asked Medina.

"I refuse to have any part of this. Make your own decisions!"

"A flare would be a smart move," said Garson. "If she went out there in the dark, they'd think it was one of us and just open fire."

"There can be nothing smart about an act of stupidity!" snapped Luac. "They will shoot her anyway."

"I weel go," she said.

"Then I'd better give her the light," said Medina.

"Suit yourself!" said Luac.

Medina found the flare gun, loaded it, turned to Maria Gomez. "*Vaya con Dios, Abuelita.*"

Go with God, little grandmother. Garson shuddered, almost called out to stop her.

Anita Luac moved up beside him. "I'm afraid!" she whispered.

Again a flare arched over the lake, swung lazily downward.

Immediately, Maria Gomez moved out the door and across the terrace, going rapidly in her curious shambling walk.

They watched her unchain the boat, clamber into it, take up the oars and begin rowing across the lake.

"I told you they wouldn't shoot!" said Garson.

"You are speaking too soon," said Luac.

The rowboat reached the halfway mark, crossed it. Suddenly, a bullet fired from the ridge splatted the water beside the boat.

"You see!" barked Luac.

Another bullet smacked into the stern of the boat at the waterline. The old woman redoubled her efforts, rowing frantically.

"You made a mistake," said Luac. "The boat is sinking!"

"The *caribe!*" said Garson. "If the boat sinks..."

"She may yet make it," said Luac. "Nita!"

"Yes, Father."

"Let Choco out the rear door. Maybe he can silence those men on the ridge."

They ran across the room, into the darkness of the hall.

"Why's Raul shooting at her?" asked Garson.

"Because it's obvious that she's going for help."

Garson looked up at the swaying flare—another ten minutes of light. "We should've shot the flare out lower!"

Another shot hit the rowboat alongside Maria, showered her with water. They recognized the sharp splat of Raul's Luger.

Now, they could see that the boat was sinking rapidly.

"Why doesn't he just kill her and be done with it?" demanded Garson.

"That's not Raul's way," said Luac. "He likes to see the *caribe* get them alive!"

Anita Luac returned from the rear of the house, stared out at the lake, turned and buried her head against Garson's chest. "I can't look!"

Another shot from the Luger smacked into the rowboat at the stern. It was followed immediately by the roar of a rifle, and another fusillade sounded from the ridge.

Less than a hundred yards separated Maria Gomez from the opposite shore.

They could see groups of men along the other dock and on the shore watching her plight. The rowboat showed less than an inch above the water, moved sluggishly in spite of the old woman's frantic efforts.

"Why don't those men over there do something?" demanded Garson.

He stared at Maria Gomez struggling beneath the blue-white torment of the flare.

"What can they do?" asked Luac. "They fear that if they go onto the lake, they will become targets."

Garson's eyes caught movement to the right, pointed. "El Grillo!"

The gnome figure of the little Mexican bent over a paddle, shooting his dugout toward the sinking rowboat.

"I think he will be too late," said Luac.

Anita Luac looked up, stared fascinated for a moment, again hid her eyes against Garson.

Something flashed silver and splashed across the foundering gunwale of the rowboat. Maria stood up, struck at it with the oar. She turned, screamed at El Grillo, who redoubled his efforts.

"Why doesn't Raul shoot at El Grillo, too?" asked Garson.

"Choco may be keeping them occupied."

Another silver flash leaped the sinking gunwale. Maria tried to climb onto the rowboat's seat. Her foot slipped, and she fell sideways into the lake. One hand reappeared, vanished.

Even from the peninsula they could see the water boil with *caribe*.

El Grillo's canoe shot across the disturbed water. He looked down once, then stared at the peninsula. A flick of his paddle turned the canoe back the way he had come.

The flare came down to the lake, seemed to hover there for a moment, then hissed into the water.

Garson stared into the darkness, a sick feeling in his stomach.

Anita Luac looked up at him, a question in her eye.

Garson shook his head.

She shuddered.

"That's torn it," said Luac. "We may all be fish food before morning!"

"I don't like the quiet on the ridge," said Garson.

"That fiend," said Anita Luac.

"Do you have any more brilliant ideas, Mr. Garson?" asked Luac.

"Shut up!" barked Garson.

As long as he lived, Garson knew he would carry that scene in his mind: the old woman struggling, falling, the water boiling with the terrible fish.

"Someone's coming," said Luac. "It's Choco."

Medina slipped in the door. "I winged Raul!"

"What're they doing up on the ridge?" asked Luac.

"They're staying put!"

"Is Raul seriously injured?"

"I don't know. He fell, but then he crawled away."

"Did you see the... lake?" asked Garson.

"I saw."

"If we could only signal El Grillo," said Garson.

"Ah, hope," said Luac. "The carrot on the stick leading us into eternity!"

"There may be a way," said Garson. "El Grillo told me to signal him with a white cloth if I wanted him to come for me."

"Well, you just go right out there and wave to him now," said Luac.

Garson ignored the jibe. "He told me to hang the cloth on a limb near that mudbank where he let me out."

"And you believe this will bring him?"

"Why not?"

"He might do it, Father," said Anita Luac.

"And the sun may rise tomorrow in the west!"

"Give me a revolver," said Garson. "I'm going to try to tie a handkerchief on one of those bushes. I'll want both hands free."

"I will do it," said Medina.

"You're wounded," said Garson. "This one's easy. It's away from the ridge where Raul and his men are."

"They could be working around behind us right now," said Medina. "I don't see why they haven't already tried."

"Maybe you discouraged them," said Garson. "Give me a revolver."

Medina went into the darkness at one side of the room, returned with a bullet-studded belt, a holster and a gun. "This is my last spare thirty-eight," he said. "Try not to lose it."

"I'll do my best," said Garson.

"And this time, aim two inches lower," said Medina.

Anita Luac came up beside Garson. "Be careful," she whispered.

"This is another stupidity!" said Luac. "El Grillo will not come for us. He may very well think we're the ones who killed his sister just now."

"Then does he believe in personal revenge?" asked Garson.

"He's Mexican!"

"Then he'll come."

"But if he thinks I…"

"He'll come," repeated Garson. "For one reason or another, he'll come. Because he has a price, or to get revenge on you—he'll come."

"Ahhhhhh," said Luac. "Now I am relegated to the role of bait! Not yet bait for the worms, but soon enough that, too, eh?"

"Do you think he could stand against four of us?" asked Garson.

"He could stand against a thousand who trusted a fool to guide them!"

"Maybe there's a better way," said Anita Luac.

"Oh, let him try," said Luac.

"Perhaps it will work," said Medina. He was staring at the shadows of the far shore. "They still are not coming."

"They've just had an object lesson on why they should stay off the lake," said Luac. He pointed to the moon-silvered hills beyond the lake. "But they will have their darkness soon. See those clouds."

They all moved closer to the window, looked at a line of black clouds moving in across the hills. "It is early for the rains," said Luac. "But this is the kind of luck we may expect!"

"What will Raul be doing now?" asked Garson.

"He is like a wounded tiger," said Medina. "He is waiting for his moment to leap from ambush!"

Garson studied the far shore. *We'll be caught like a nut in the jaws of a nutcracker if we don't get out of here before Raul's men come down from the ridge and across the lake! And if they catch us on the lake...*

He shuddered.

"The sooner the better," said Medina.

Garson buckled the cartridge belt around his waist, settled the revolver in its holster.

"As soon as I get back, we can shoot up another flare so El Grillo will see the signal."

"For luck," said Anita Luac. She handed him a white scarf. "Tie that to the bush!"

"The knight goes forth!" muttered Luac.

Garson stood by the door for a moment. The moonlight on the terrace suddenly seemed to take on the brightness of a searchlight.

"Stay low and hug the wall," said Medina.

Garson nodded, slipped outside, crouched and ran to the right, paused in the shadows at the corner of the house. The muggy warmth of the night seemed to hold a special menace. He steeled himself against the fear that tortured his nerves, moved back along the house to the garden wall, paused.

The sounds of the insects came to him amplified out of all proportion by his fear-tuned senses. He crouched, crossed an open space to the shadows of a line of bushes, felt the sand of the trail under his feet.

Stealthily, listening at every step, he worked his way down the trail to the lakeshore. He came to the log where he had hidden the empty revolver, froze as he thought he heard movement behind him. The darkness revealed nothing.

He turned back to the lake. It lay before him smooth as a piece of luminescent oiled silk. The far shore was a bank of grotesque shadows between the lake and the moon-silvered hills.

Garson stepped forward, bent back a limb of a bush at his side and let it whip back into place. He crouched, fearful of the noise his movements had produced. And now, he noticed with an abrupt choking sensation of fear that the sounds of the insects behind him had taken on an irregular pattern. It was like the movement of a zone of silence toward him.

With infinite care, Garson stooped, crawled forward, drew his revolver and stretched out behind the rotten log.

Something grated on the sand of the trail.

Light exploded above the lake.

Garson cursed under his breath, believing in that moment that Luac had betrayed him. Then he saw the pattern of falling sparks from the rocket. They formed a zig-zag tracing back to the ridge above the hacienda.

We're not the only ones with flares!

The bushes above Garson cast a meager shadow. He tried to move farther back into the obscurity, froze at a low voice from the swamp on his left.

"Ah, Mr. Garson!"

Raul Separdo! Garson tried to probe the blackness of the swamp, saw only twisting shadows and the reflection of the flare from glistening leaves.

"Drop your gun, Mr. Garson."

The low voice, despite its emotionless flatness, carried the heaviest threat that Garson had ever heard. His fingers seemed to open of their own accord. The revolver plopped into the leaves.

Separdo, dragging his left foot in a twisting limp, came out of the swamp, crossed to a position beside Garson, bent and retrieved the revolver.

"Now, we will wait for Choco to come to the rescue," said Separdo.

He grinned down at Garson, his face like a hole-pierced mask in the blue-white glare.

Separdo's alone, thought Garson. *One of those dugouts couldn't hold more than three persons. Choco accounted for one of them. Someone on the ridge fired the flare. That means one against one here if I can trick him off guard!*

"Be very cautious about your movements," whispered Separdo. He backed away from Garson into the shadows of the bushes. Separdo's left leg dragged heavily. He grimaced at every step.

A wounded tiger!

Garson looked up the sanded line of the trail. *Choco will come! He'll wait for a reasonable length of time, then he'll come searching.* He twisted his head very slowly, looked up at the dazzling brilliance of the flare. It had been fired lower than the others, but there was still five minutes of light. *Maybe Choco will wait for the darkness.*

Evidently Separdo had the same idea. He whispered from the darkness: "Choco will wait until the light is gone. But I have the ears of a cat, my friend. Do not disturb the leaves around you. And when Choco comes, give no warning, or my first bullets will be for you!"

Garson swallowed in sick impotence, abruptly recalled the empty revolver he had hidden beneath this log. He guessed the position of it to almost where his left hand rested on the leaves. Slowly, Garson moved his hand into the damp earth beneath the log. The leaves rustled.

"What are you doing?" hissed Separdo.

"Something crawling up my sleeve," whispered Garson.

"Perhaps a scorpion," said Separdo. "Leave it alone."

Garson's questing hand encountered only the earth.

The shadows from the flare crept across the ground, darkness blotted out the scene.

Garson's heart hammered. He could feel clammy perspiration running down his jaw line, down his neck, along his sides. It felt like so many running insects.

A twig snapped in the darkness.

Separdo's Luger dug into Garson's side.

Someone went "Hsssst!" from the swamp side.

The Luger dug deeper.

Garson moved his left hand along under the log, fighting to hide the motion. He had no idea what he would do with the empty gun when he found it, only felt the great need of it in his hand.

Above him, Separdo went "Hssssst!"

An answering sound came from the swamp.

Garson's hand encountered cold metal.

The Luger was removed from his side. He felt rather than heard Separdo move back.

The revolver came out from under the log with only the faintest rustling of a leaf. It felt crusted under his hand, and he wondered if it would work even if he managed to get bullets from his belt and into the cylinder.

Footsteps grated on the trail beside the log.

The Luger cracked in a blue spurt of flame above Garson's head, was answered by the roar of Medina's revolver.

Two bodies collided above Garson. A foot dug into his back, was gone. Garson shook the revolver, broke it open, dug frantically for cartridges, fumbled them into the cylinder, closed it.

A loud sound came from directly ahead of Garson. Medina cursed. There came a moment of silence. The circle of a small penlight dug a hole out of the night, revealed Medina on hands and knees feeling across the ground for his revolver. The dim figure of Separdo stood outlined behind the light, the Luger held in his right hand.

The light flicked once across Garson's face, back to Medina.

"Do you want it like that, Choco?" asked Separdo. He chuckled. "Or will you try running and give me a moving target?"

Garson said a silent prayer that no earth clogged the revolver. He brought it up, squeezed the trigger. He seemed to feel the kick of the gun in his hand before he heard the shot.

Separdo stumbled backward. The penlight in his hand described a slow arc from the ground up across the bushes. He sprawled sideways off the trail. The light fell, was extinguished.

There came the sound of swift movement from Medina's position, then his voice: "Garson?"

"Yes?"

"You got him!"

"Is he dead? Check! Are you all right, Choco?"

"Yes. He missed me." Medina came closer. "Again I owe you a debt, *Señor.*"

"No, Choco. This was one that took both of us." He explained what happened, speaking quickly in a low voice.

Medina laughed softly, gripped Garson's arm. "Now, I will teach you a trick. If one pushes a limb ahead of one along a trail like this where it will make noise, the sound will hide one's own passing, and never give the true position!"

Garson recalled the grating sound on the trail just before Separdo fired, seemed to hear Luac's voice saying: *"Choco knows many bad tricks!"*

At the house, Luac accepted their story with only a grunt when they said Separdo was dead.

Anita Luac dug her fingers into Garson's arm while he spoke. Her face in the moonlight revealed a wide-eyed elation.

"I shouldn't be glad," she whispered. "But I am!"

"There's still one of them on the ridge," said Medina.

"Leave him," said Luac. "The clouds will be across the moon in a few minutes. Get the flare pistol ready." He bent over the machine gun, smoothed the cartridge belt.

Garson took up a rifle, moved to the window ledge beside Luac, sat down and rested the rifle across the broken glass. Anita Luac took up a position beside him with another rifle.

"There's movement along the shore," said Medina.

"Where?" asked Luac.

"Down toward the printing plant. They may be trying to get some more men around the edge."

"Try a few shots with the rifle, Mr. Garson," said Luac. "We do not want them to know yet about the Lewis gun."

Garson brought up his rifle, aimed it into the blackness down the lake, squeezed off one shot. Immediately, a crackling of return fire came from directly across the lake. He got off two more shots before ducking behind the window, heard Anita's rifle fire once. She crouched down beside him.

Antone Luac's voice came from the shadows. "Olaf's force is across there. They are organized and well directed."

"I fear you're right, *Patron*," said Medina.

"That toad!" said Anita Luac.

Garson watched the moonlight fading from the floor behind the window, lifted his head, stared across the lake. An occasional rifle shot still sparked from the opposite shore. He heard bullets slam into the adobe wall, felt curiously immune to them, as though the darkness were a shield.

The moon became a misty luminescence behind the clouds, grew darker, darker. The lake faded into blackness.

"Now we count off a couple of minutes," said Luac.

"Give them three minutes," said Medina. They heard him counting under his breath.

The seconds passed like hours. They could hear a faint whispering of sound on the lake.

"Let there be light!" said Luac.

The rocket arched into the darkness, exploded to hissing brilliance. The light revealed a long line of canoes out from the far shore, paddles frozen for one instant like a great tableau. Then several back-paddled. Others shot their canoes ahead. The heavy cracking of rifles punctuated by spurts of flame winked along the shore behind the canoes.

"Now!" snapped Medina.

The Lewis gun flamed and roared beside Garson. Its bullets started at the far left, swept across the canoes like a deadly scythe.

The rifle fire from the shore stopped as though in shock, then came on with a redoubled crescendo. Bullets smacked all along the wall, around the window, against the back wall of the room.

Garson pushed Anita down below the window ledge, held his own gaze fascinated on the scene across the lake.

The Lewis gun began a second deadly traverse through the shattered canoes, then lifted to the shore.

"Another belt, Choco," said Luac.

"*Sí, Patron.*"

Garson could smell paint blistering from the window ledge near the gun barrel as it concentrated on one grouping of rifle flamings.

Again the machine gun traversed the far shore.

Now, there were only sporadic shots from the darkness across the lake.

"I wonder what Olaf is thinking now?" said Luac. He stopped firing.

The lake across from them was a scene of madness: overturned canoes, floundering and screaming men, the deadly boiling of the *caribe* through the water.

They could see a few men make it to the opposite dock. Others fell back, sank from sight.

"They will not try that again soon," said Luac.

"It's horrible!" said Anita.

Garson became conscious that she had straightened, was staring at the lake as fascinated as he.

"Now, I will tell you something," said Luac. "What we have just done makes it absolutely necessary that none of us is captured alive.

Garson stared at him. "What?"

"*Sí*," muttered Medina. He looked down at Anita Luac. "*Señorita, you* must not let them take you." He shifted his attention to Garson. "If it becomes necessary, save one bullet for the *Señorita* and one for yourself, Mr. Garson."

"What are you talking about?"

"Choco and I have seen the peon legions in action," said Luac. "We will all keep in mind that it would be a kindness to my daughter and to ourselves if…"

"Stop it, Father!"

"Yes, my dear." His voice was strangely gentle.

Medina stirred restlessly. "This is not like Queretero, eh, *Patron?*"

"No, Choco. Then we had Pancho telling us what to do."

"I do not think we have much time, *Patron.*"

"I was thinking the same thing, Choco. This is a long gamble. I will spike the machine gun now."

Garson stared at the shadowy figure of Luac. "Spike the…"

"We must go down to the lake," said Medina. "If El Grillo comes, we must be there."

"What if *they* shoot up a flare?" asked Garson.

"I do not believe they want light," said Luac. "Eh, Choco?"

"That is my thought, *Patron.*"

Luac said, "There! They will not use this weapon!" He stood up, turned away into the darkness at the rear of the house. "Excuse me one moment."

"Listen!" hissed Garson.

They became very still.

The murmuring of many voices came from across the lake.

"How many men over there, Choco?"

"They could muster perhaps three hundred. I think we caught about half of them on the lake."

Antone Luac returned, his shoulder bent under a heavy suitcase. Medina took it from him.

"Our insurance policy," said Luac.

The manuscripts! thought Garson.

"Stay close behind me," said Medina.

Garson hung a bandolier of rifle cartridges over his shoulder, slung a rifle over the bandolier. Anita came up beside him, slipped her hand in his.

"Do you hear something on the lake?" asked Luac.

"I think they are making another try, *Patron.*"

"So soon!"

"I believe they are angry, *Patron*. Were I directing them, I would make the rush silently in a body, and detail men to shoot down another flare if we try to light up the lake."

"This is not good," whispered Luac. "Garson! Remember what I said about them taking us alive!"

"Let us go," said Medina.

They slipped out the front door into the thick warmth of the night. Now they could hear faint splashings on the lake.

Garson felt the trail underfoot, saw the ghostly movement of Medina ahead, felt Anita's palm moist against his own. Her silence was like a resignation, a giving up of hope.

At the lakeshore, they crouched in the bushes. The heavy moisture of the night seemed to close in on them, crawling with the movement of insects.

Antone Luac put his mouth close to Garson's ear, whispered: "If someone other than *El Grillo* comes, we must try to take the canoes silently."

Garson patted the old man's shoulder to show that he understood.

A soft splash sounded from the lake directly ahead of them. Garson tensed. It could have been a fish, or a piece of dirt dropping from the bank. He put Anita's hand into her father's, slipped forward.

Directly beneath him a soft voice whispered: "*Señor* Garson?"

"Yes."

Now he could make out a dim movement of white, the darker blot of a log canoe on the lake.

"It is El Grillo," whispered the voice. "I saw your signal. Are you alone?"

"No. The Luacs and Choco are with me."

"That was my guess. I brought two canoes."

Medina whispered in Garson's ear, voice so low that Garson had to strain to hear it. "I smell a trap. Be very careful!"

Garson tried to ignore the hammering of his heart. He reached back for Anita, drew her forward and passed her down to El Grillo's canoe.

A door slammed at the hacienda. They froze to waiting stillness.

Medina hissed, "Quickly!" He helped Luac down to the spare canoe, handed him the heavy suitcase of manuscripts.

Garson slipped into the front of El Grillo's canoe, saw Medina take the stern of the other. Side by side, they pushed into the lake, turned right along the shore.

Louder sounds came from the hacienda. A powerful flashlight speared into the lake along the dock. Someone cursed. The light was extinguished.

The two canoes skimmed into the upper curve of the lake, moving with fewer than six feet between them.

Abruptly, El Grillo whispered, "Wait!"

Paddles dug into the water. The canoes stopped, drifted.

Garson experienced a sudden sense of extreme menace, glanced back at the dim figure of El Grillo in the stern. El Grillo turned to the other canoe.

"*Patron*," he said.

"What is it, Grillito?"

"I have some questions, *Patron*."

"Later!" hissed Medina.

Garson stared at the other canoe coasting slowly beside them, the darker shadows of the swamp edge behind it.

"This is a shotgun in my lap," said El Grillo. "It has a hair trigger. It is pointed at you."

Anita gasped. Their canoe tipped, steadied.

"Who killed my nephew, Eduardo?" demanded El Grillo.

"Raul Separdo, you fool!" said Luac.

Garson slipped his revolver from its holster, slowly moved it around until it pointed past Anita toward El Grillo.

"And who shot the boat from under my sister?" demanded El Grillo.

"Don't be an idiot!" said Medina. "You know it was Raul!"

"Perhaps you ordered both of them to be killed, *Patron*!"

"No!" said Anita.

"I have you covered with my gun, El Grillo," said Garson. "Drop your shotgun over the side!"

"You are a child," said El Grillo. "I could still sink the other canoe even with your bullet in me. The *caribe* would do the rest. The recoil of my gun would overturn this canoe unless I was here to prevent it with my paddle."

Antone Luac said, "Stop this nonsense, Grillito!"

"I do not think it is nonsense, *Patron*." Again Garson felt the canoe shift and steady under him. "I give you a choice: You two will swim ashore in the swamp. Your daughter and the foolish gringo I will take to my barrio and help to escape."

"That's no choice," said Garson.

Anita said, "My father's telling you the truth!"

"You, of course, would say so," said El Grillo.

Garson glanced back toward the hacienda, saw lights glowing now in the windows, the movement of many people on the lakeshore. He looked across at the other canoe, thought of how quickly the *caribe* would swarm, attracted by Medina's wound.

"You know Raul gave the orders around here," said Luac. "You know we were his prisoners!"

"So you say, *Patron*."

"And I have already killed Raul for you," said Garson. "You should realize that we're not lying. The shots that sank your sister's boat came from the ridge beyond the hacienda. You know Raul was up there."

"Why would Raul kill my nephew?" asked El Grillo.

Garson sensed that the man was weakening, knew that the time they were losing could be fatal. "He found out that Eduardo was responsible for my coming here. Eduardo was working with me to rescue the Luacs."

"Then why did Raul kill my sister?"

"Because he was afraid that she had discovered who killed Eduardo and was crossing the lake to tell you!"

"Let us waste no more time. If we stay here, we die. I shall take the chance and believe you," said El Grillo. "Your words ring of truth." His paddle dipped into the lake. The canoe shot ahead.

Garson felt faint with relief. Anita bent forward, gripped his arm until it hurt.

The canoes approached the log raft at the barrio.

Without warning, they were bathed in the glare of a powerful spotlight. From the darkness at one side came a guttural voice.

"Good evening, Antone."

Luac grunted, "Olaf!"

Garson lifted one hand to shield his eyes from the light.

A squat, fat man waddled into the field of the light. He wore dark trousers, an orange shirt with a pink bandanna at the throat, a dark beret. His face was dominated by the wide gash of a thick-lipped mouth, slitted eyes. The nose and chin were porcine, but the total effect was—as Anita had said—that of a toad.

"I knew that if you got through you would come for the car," said Olaf. He turned to the other canoe. "Ah, Nita! As lovely as ever, I see. And this would be the ingenious Mr. Hal Garson." He nodded. "Quite a cargo you have, Grillo."

Garson sensed a total cessation of activity across the lake at the hacienda, turned, saw men lining the shore there, rifles raised.

Olaf lifted a hand from his side, revealed a machine pistol. "Such a bitter parting for old friends," he said.

El Grillo shifted in the stern of the canoe. "Olaf!"

"Yes, Grillo?"

"You may have the gringo here and the girl, but Choco and the old man are mine!"

"Oh? And what makes you think I want those two?"

"You will have questions for Mr. Garson. And I believe you will have other uses for the *Señorita.*"

"It does seem a shame to waste such beauty on the *caribe,*" said Olaf. "But you do not appear in a position to bargain, Grillo."

"I think you want these two," said El Grillo. "What happens to them if I tip over the canoe?"

Olaf turned his toad face to Antone Luac. "This has become quite interesting, don't you think, Antone?"

Luac remained silent, breathing heavily.

"Why are Choco and Mr. Luac so important to you, Grillo?"

"They killed Eduardo. They killed Maria!"

"Then why did you bring them across the lake?"

"To bring them so close to what they would lose!"

Olaf guffawed. "How Mexican!"

"I think I will paddle back to the hacienda now," said El Grillo. "The men over there will know how to treat the gringo and the *Señorita*."

"Wait!" Olaf sounded amused.

Garson moved his hand toward his revolver.

"Careful!" said Olaf. The muzzle of the machine pistol came up, stared at him like an unwinking eye.

"Choco and the old man are mine to do with as I please?" asked El Grillo.

Olaf nodded. "Yes."

El Grillo's paddle dipped into the water, turned the canoe slightly to the left. The machine pistol still stared at Garson.

A roaring "No!" came from Medina.

Out of the corner of his eye, Garson saw Medina's hand blur toward his pistol, knew that the big Mexican would be too late even as he saw the machine pistol swing toward the other canoe.

A double roar came from behind Garson, tipping the canoe until the gunwale shipped water. El Grillo raised the shotgun.

Olaf staggered, walked forward on tiptoe, the machine pistol slipping from his hands. He fell face down into the water, a great patch of red across the back of his orange shirt. Silver forms darted in the shallows. One of Olaf's outstretched hands moved.

"We must hurry!" said El Grillo. He shot the canoe forward to the log raft.

Garson could hear shouts from the lake, turned, saw the canoes nearly halfway across. A rifle barked from one of the forward canoes. A geyser of mud kicked up beside the crude dock. Garson lifted his own rifle from the canoe bottom, leaped to the dock and began firing slowly, picking targets.

Medina's revolver barked once. The spotlight shattered, plunging the shore into darkness.

The line of canoes halted, retreated. More shots flashed from the canoes and from the far shore. Garson heard bullets strike the ground around them.

The others scrambled onto the raft-dock. They all ran for the limousine.

Garson heard Luac say, "Grillo, take the mountain road! Head for Guadalajara!"

The limousine roared and skidded as El Grillo sent it rushing out of the barrio and down the track that Garson had climbed in the heat.

Once, a horseman come out of the brush behind them, whirled and shot at the fleeing car. Medina leaned precariously out of his window, fired back until the man plunged his horse into the brush.

They stopped once in the night at a sleeping village. Lightning forked the sky around them, and thunder rolled. Somewhere, a horse whinnied in terror.

El Grillo routed out a sleepy woman who filled their gas tank from standing barrels. And again they were off down the road to Guadalajara.

The time passed in a plunging of headlights through the night—between the scaling mud walls of villages, across cobblestones, several times bumping over the railroad tracks that had carried Garson to Ciudad Brockman—and eventually onto a paved highway that speared across the highlands.

Garson took the ride in a kind of somnolent retreat, filled with suspicions and anger, with self-recriminations. He thought he slept at one point, but he was not sure. The events of the day and night seemed to have drained him of the ability to follow his own emotions.

The big limousine bounced across a rutted stretch of highway without slackening speed, splashed through a mudhole. El Grillo drove like a marionette with quick movements of his thin hands. The night rushed past the car.

From his seat in the right rear of the limousine, Garson stared at the back of El Grillo's neck. Choco Medina, beside El Grillo, turned and spoke to the little driver. The closed glass between the two sections effectively blanked out the conversation.

Ahead, Garson could see the lights of Guadalajara reflected from low lying clouds. There had been rain, but now the air was clear with the fresh washed aftermath of the downpour and the danger.

Anita sat stiffly beside Garson, her father on the other side. All during the ride from Ciudad Brockman she had refused conversation. A mocking light had been strong in her eyes.

Garson felt the sick stirring of anger within him.

I've had it! They've used me and no longer need me!

"Where'll we go in Guadalajara?" asked Garson.

Luac glanced at him. "We will take you to the airport and then be on our way."

"Will I ever see you again?"

"Probably not."

153

The events of the past days were beginning to take on a new pattern in Garson's mind. He said, "Maria Gomez spoke good English."

"Excellent English," said Luac.

"So did Eduardo."

"Of the finest," said Luac. "He…" He broke off.

"Who wrote that pidgin English letter?" demanded Garson.

"One of my better creations!" said Luac.

"Why did you choose me?" demanded Garson.

"You were recommended by… friends."

Garson felt the papers under this shirt, the list of names and addresses. "One of the contacts on the list you gave me?"

"As a matter of fact, yes. What do you intend to do with that list, Mr. Garson?"

"I intend to give it to the F.B.I."

"How noble of you."

"Why don't you two be quiet?" said Anita.

"We're just having a last pleasant conversation," said Luac.

"Why did you want me to *discover* you?" asked Garson.

"Well, the original plan was for us to attract you to Ciudad Brockman. Then I was to stumble upon you in the city, give you my story to get rid of you—reluctantly, of course, and…"

"But why?"

"Very simple. We didn't think we could escape from the hacienda. But we knew if they moved us, we could probably get away—especially with Choco helping. You understand that escape had become necessary? Raul was… well, you saw."

"Very neat."

"I thought so at the time. Then you blundered in with your mouth and tipped the whole show. Raul's spies alerted him. He confined me to the hacienda. He eliminated Eduardo, tried to eliminate you with that chunk of concrete. It became horribly mixed up!"

"Indeed it did. So this whole thing was a scheme to expose your hiding place and force them to move you!"

"Clever, eh?"

"Absolutely! I imagine that Eduardo and Maria Gomez—wherever they are—are just bubbling with admiration!"

"Fortunes of war!"

A strange coughing sound came from Anita. She put a hand to her face.

Garson glanced at her, returned his attention to the shadowy figure of her father. In that moment, Garson felt a complete hate and revulsion toward Luac.

He's an utter monster!

"Are you still going to write your story?" asked Luac.

"About you?"

"What else?" He chuckled. "It should make an interesting article."

Garson shook his head. "Not an article. Non-fiction couldn't do it justice." The thought captured Garson's interest. "Yes, I believe I'll do this one as fiction. It wouldn't help the general peace of mind to know that a monster like you exists anywhere except in a writer's fevered imagination."

This seemed to bother Luac. He said, "But you came to get an article!"

"I was lured here to suit a madman's whim!"

"Do it!" Luac's face set into grim lines. He fell silent.

Anita glanced up at Garson, looked away.

God help me! he thought. *I still want her! And there is no hope for me. She's cut in the same terrible pattern as her father.*

Luac shifted his position. "I would advise you never to come back to Mexico, Garson."

"Why?"

"The friends of those we killed on the lake."

"Won't they be after your skin, too?"

"Yes, but I have a million places to go. I think you will be safe if you stay away from the border."

"You think? Won't there be some big investigation of this? Won't I be questioned about my part in it?"

"Hah! The authorities will never learn about it—officially, that is. The friends of those we killed will want secrecy as much as we do."

"What about your friend, the colonel of police at Ciudad Brockman?"

"Bartolomé? He sees no evil, hears no evil, tells no evil! That might involve work. And there'd certainly be no money in it. I will see that Bartolomé gets the job of selling the hacienda. It will mean a tidy profit for him. He will see that a prospective buyer finds nothing to disturb him."

Garson sat back in a silent rage. *What a monster!*

El Grillo lifted his right hand, opened the glass partition. "*Patron.*"

Luac leaned forward.

El Grillo indicated a white sign ahead that pointed left—the airport. Garson could see the flashing lights on signal towers in the distance. The car slowed.

"Ah, yes," said Luac. He settled back, glanced at his wrist-watch. "One-forty A.M. Excellent time from Ciudad Brockman."

The limousine turned left toward the towers, presently stopped before a spotlighted stone building with a wide ramp leading up to the front. Garson experienced a sudden feeling of unreality—as though this visible evidence of civilization were false, nowhere near as actual as the hacienda and the lake from which they had escaped.

But he felt also that the events of the night had taken place in another century: long, long ago, and in another country.

And something made him recall the lines from *The Jew of Malta*: "But that was in another country, and besides the wench is dead."

He kept his eyes from looking at Anita Luac, got out of the car, heard her follow.

Luac slapped his knees. "Well, here we are!" He slid across the seat, looked up at Garson. "We'll wait while you check on the next flight. Perhaps you'll need a ride into Guadalajara. Do you have money?"

"I have checks and a letter of credit."

Now, he permitted himself to glance at Anita Luac. She stood beside the front door of the limousine, a wan look on her face, staring up at the stone building of the airport. She had never looked more beautiful to Garson—nor more desirable... nor more distant.

Anita turned, avoided his eyes, bent toward her father. "Do you think the coffee shop's open?"

"It used to stay open all night. Are you hungry?"

"I need some coffee." She reached in, took a purse from a pocket on the back of the front seat, opened it, glanced inside. "Give me some more money, Father."

"Why?"

"I'm going to buy Mr. Garson's ticket."

Sudden anger flared in Garson. "Don't put yourself to any trouble!"

She smiled with the open lift of mockery. "This is the least we can do for you."

"I'll buy my own ticket and be happily shut of you!"

"Let her have her own way," said Luac. "I've seen this mood before." He pressed a roll of bills into her purse.

She turned, patted Garson's cheek. "Don't try to stop me, darling. I shall make the most dreadful scene if you do." She went up the ramp and into the airport building.

"I'll buy you a cup of coffee," said Luac. He got out of the car, stretched.

"Your sudden generosity overwhelms me."

Choco Medina opened his door, emerged. The big Mexican's mustache drooped forlornly. Lines of fatigue were etched into his pockmarked face. He looked like a morose St. Bernard.

"We will not likely see each other again," he said.

Garson nodded. "That's one thing I regret."

"How touching," murmured Luac.

Garson put out his hand, shook with Medina. "Thanks for everything, Choco."

"It is I who am indebted to you, *Señor.*"

"Shall we be going?" snapped Luac. "Choco, you and El Grillo wait here."

"*Sí, Patron.*" He saluted Garson. "*Adiosito*... Hal."

Garson blinked, experienced a sudden choked feeling. He turned away quickly, followed Luac into the building. They crossed an almost empty lobby, entered the brightly lit coffee shop.

A scattering of airport personnel sat at the tables, several men in business suits looking tired and bored. Large windows at one side gave a view of two spotlighted planes, men working around them.

Garson and Luac took a corner table. A tired-eyed waitress crossed to them.

Luac held up three fingers. *"Tres cafes."*

She nodded, went back across the room.

Garson felt the drained-out limpness of fatigue in his muscles, the sick bitterness of frustration.

They used me, by God!

Anita came in looking distantly poised, sat down across from Garson. "Your plane leaves in an hour and half."

"You two needn't stay and hold my hand."

"Oh, but we want to." She took an envelope from her purse, put it on the table in front of Garson. "Your ticket."

"Thanks. Thanks loads!" The bitter anger overcame his control. He pushed himself away from the table, surged to his feet. "Why don't you shove off?"

"Tired of us so soon, darling?" she murmured.

Luac was studying his daughter with a puzzled expression.

Garson stepped around the table, glared down at her. The mockery in her eyes was suddenly washed away by something that seemed to stare out at him from some deep well. She got to her feet, looked up at him.

"What're you waiting for?" demanded Garson.

"Perhaps I forgot something," she whispered.

He felt that they were suddenly in a vacuum—the murmurous coffee shop sounds around them did not exist. The curious glances of the other patrons were nothing to him.

There were only these two people, Garson and Anita Luac, in a moment frozen out of time.

"Maybe you did forget something." He reached with savage violence, jerked her to him, crushing his mouth onto hers. She accepted the kiss without resistance, without response.

Garson pushed her away. "Is that what you forgot?"

She shook her head from side to side. The look on her face, the light in her eyes, made him think of a diabolic Madonna.

Her arms went around his neck. She pressed against him, lifted her lips, stared up at his eyes.

Garson found that he could not resist.

The kiss shook him with desire and bitterness. It made him think of the garden behind the hacienda, of all the empty years ahead of him without her.

She pulled away, whispered softly, "That is what I forgot."

He took a shuddering breath, noted abruptly that Antone Luac had disappeared from the table. "Couldn't your father stand to look at our parting?"

Anita shook her head, held up her hand. Her fingers grasped an envelope. "He saw what he accomplished."

"Saw what?"

"My ticket."

It was like a dash of cold water across the face. "Your tick..."

"Don't you want me to go with you?"

All he could do was nod. Then: "Why did you do it like this?"

A look of sadness and infinite regret crossed her face. "I didn't know how to tell him." She shrugged, and something very like anger replaced the sadness in her face. "I fought this dreadful scheme of his from the first. I knew it would come to no good." Her eyes seemed to burn into Garson's. "He destroyed everything I loved. The hacienda—I can never return! And poor old Maria…" She shook her head, shuddered.

"Do you trust me on such short notice, Nita?"

"I trust my instincts about you." Her mocking smile returned, touched only faintly by something wistful. "I make my own decisions, you know."

"I love you, Nita."

"And I love you." She turned her head away, spoke with a slow distinctness. "I don't want to be like my father: bitter and unhappy. I want to be like me." She looked back at Garson. "And I never knew what it was like to be me until that night in the grove when we kissed."

"Is that when…"

Someone coughed beside them.

They turned. A young man in an attendant's uniform extended an envelope to Anita, leered at Garson. She took the envelope. The young man saluted, departed.

Her hands made nervous, fumbling motions opening the envelope. She pulled out a note, glanced at it, then read it aloud with a husky sadness in her voice:

"You will never be able to find me. I am going with Choco and El Grillo. The enclosed claim check is for your insurance, which I have prepaid through on your tickets. There should be enough money in what I gave you to see you to the States where it is my belief that your young man will take care of matters. He is a fool, but a dependable one according to all reports. If things turn out badly, cash in some of the insurance. Please do not name any of your little fools after me."

She folded the note, bent over the table, pushed the paper into her purse.

Garson saw tears slipping down her cheeks. "We can still catch him, Nita." He turned toward the lobby.

"No!" She caught his arm. "He's already gone. The ground will swallow them."

"But, after all, he is your father! Won't you ever hear…"

"Be calm, darling," she murmured, and the infinite sadness was plain in her voice. "We will hear from my father when he has found a new place to hide."

ABOUT THE AUTHOR

Frank Herbert, the visionary author of *Dune*, wrote more than twenty other novels, including *Hellstrom's Hive, The White Plague, The Green Brain,* and *The Dosadi Experiment.* During his life, he received great acclaim for his sweeping vision and the deep philosophical underpinnings in his writings. His life is detailed in the Hugo-nominated biography *Dreamer of Dune,* by Brian Herbert.

Other Frank Herbert novels available from WordFire Press include *Destination: Void, The Heaven Makers, Direct Descent, The Godmakers,* and three previously unpublished novels, *High-Opp, Angels' Fall,* and *A Game of Authors.* Also available are *The Pandora Sequence,* which includes *The Jesus Incident, The Lazarus Effect,* and *The Ascension Factor* (all with Bill Ransom), and Herbert's last-published novel, *Man of Two Worlds,* coauthored with his son Brian.

WordFire Press Books

by Frank Herbert

Angels' Fall
Destination: Void
Direct Descent
The Godmakers
The Heaven Makers
High-Opp
Soul Catcher

by Frank Herbert and Bill Ransom

The Jesus Incident
The Lazarus Effect
The Ascension Factor
The Pandora Sequence (omnibus)

by Frank Herbert and Brian Herbert

Man of Two Worlds

And be sure to read the compelling biography of Frank Herbert, **Dreamer of Dune,** by Brian Herbert, for insight into one of the greatest minds in science fiction.

CPSIA information can be obtained at www.ICGtesting.com
Printed in the USA
LVOW11s1038270214

375280LV00030B/554/P